HEIRESS
TO LOVE

Donna Bell

Zebra Books
Kensington Publishing Corp.
http://www.zebrabooks.com

ZEBRA BOOKS are published by

Kensington Publishing Corp.
850 Third Avenue
New York, NY 10022

First Printing: June, 2000
10 9 8 7 6 5 4 3 2 1

Printed in the United States of America

×

To Hallie,
whose publication date was 1999.
And to David and Jamie, for giving
me my wonderful granddaughter.

ONE

The letter slipped to the floor unheeded by the reader, but the listener regarded her sister's blanched complexion and swooped down to retrieve the missive, her expression changing with the rapidity of a pendulum, swinging from fear, to delight, and back again to fear as she read.

"What does this mean?" she asked breathlessly before recalling her sister's state of shock and adding solicitously, "Missy, do sit down before you faint."

"I never faint," said the elder of the two, pushing away her sister's hasty offering of wine, but seeking the nearest chair. "And I have no need of spirits to give me Dutch courage."

"I know, but it is such a shock."

"Not at all, Felicity. Since the reading of Papa's will—what is it now, two years?—we have known something like this would happen." Her bleak expression belied the cool indifference of her tone.

"But not this, not exactly. I don't know what to think," said Felicity, perusing the letter once more and shaking her pretty blond curls in amazement. "A Season," she added reverently.

"Yes, a Season!" said Missy, her disgust at the

thought palpable. "It is ludicrous! Here am I, three and twenty, and suddenly I must go to London and answer to the whims of some old man whom I've never even met!" She drew her booted feet up under her on the chair and hunched her shoulders, biting at her lower lip and frowning fiercely.

"Surely he cannot be so very old, Missy. He only just sold out his commission in the army," protested the younger girl, her blond curls hiding her face as she bent her head to read the letter yet again.

"What has that to say to the matter? Old or young, he has some nerve—ordering us to London for the Season, indeed. I cannot think of leaving now! Why, I've still got a million things to do to get King's Shilling ready for the track!" said Missy Lambert, burying her head in her hands, while her mind worked feverishly on some practical solution.

"Perhaps you can bring King to London with us?"

"He's not ready for that at all! He still tries to bolt at the sight of a whip. Besides, that is not the point, Felicity. Don't you understand? What we wish to do, or wish not to do, is no longer our decision. It is this guardian we have been saddled with, this Garrett Wyndridge. Why, I only met the man once, and that was years and years ago. I still can't fathom why Papa chose him, of all people."

"It's Sir Garrett, Missy, and it is a Season," whispered Felicity, gripping the letter.

"Yes, a Season," echoed Missy Lambert dismally.

How happy she had been when her papa had agreed that a Season was a frivolous expense. Missy had cared nothing for it, much preferring her horses and the stables to balls and candlelight. And a good thing it had been. She would never have been successful at flirting and simpering. But now, thanks to her father's inane notion that his eldest daughter would not be able to continue running the stables as she had been for the last five years, *now* she was to have her Season.

Missy looked up to find her sister smiling dreamily. She squared her shoulders and skewered Felicity with a militant glare. "I won't go; that's all there is to it."

"Not go?" squeaked the younger Miss Lambert, leaping to her feet, starting toward her sister, shaking the letter at her before stopping, pivoting, and taking herself back to her chair. "If you're sure?" She essayed a brave smile in answer to her sister's decisive nod. "Then I shan't go either," Felicity said solemnly.

"Right, then it's back to normal for us," said Missy, uncrossing her booted feet and rising. "I told the squire he could bring his broodmares over for Harry."

"Lord Harry? I thought he was getting a bit past it."

"Devil a bit," replied Missy, picking a piece of hay off her riding breeches. With an unladylike stretch, she grinned at her younger sister and replaced her cap on her head, carefully tucking in every strand of brown hair that had escaped its pins. "All I want is to be able to finish training King's Shilling. He is my horse, not the new heir's, and when he wins the big purse at Newmarket, we'll be set. We will be free of this upstart Papa saw fit to saddle us with."

"I do hope you are right, Missy," said Felicity, a note of wistfulness creeping into her voice.

"I know I am; if I can make King's Shilling forget

his past, forget his fears, he can beat every other horse in England. He is that fast," said her elder sister, slapping her thigh with the riding crop she carried. Missy favored her sister with a smile of great bravado before sauntering out through the terrace doors.

She paused on the stone steps a moment, looking beyond the small gardens at the expanse of green paddocks dotted with mares and early foals. "I have to be right," she whispered.

Inside, Felicity's rose-colored gown swirled delicately around her ankles as she made her way to the escritoire and whittled a sharp point on her pen. Dipping it in the ink, she paused to consider before writing:

Dear Cousin Garrett,

While we are cognizant of the honor you do us in inviting us to London for the Season, I fear we must decline. Yorkshire may seem very rustic to you, but it is our home, and we are quite happy here. Thank you again.

Your humble servant,

Biting at her lower lip, Felicity hesitated. To sign her sister's name would be dishonest, but to leave the letter of their new guardian unanswered was the height of poor manners. She could sign it herself, but that would not alleviate the need for Missy, the elder sister, to write her own letter. And if there was one thing Felicity felt certain about, it was that her obstinate sister had absolutely no intention of responding to Sir Garrett Wyndridge's summons.

Sighing over this difficulty, Felicity brightened and finished the letter by writing Missy's name followed by her own. Satisfied, she addressed and sealed the envelope, then slipped it into the pocket of her apron before returning to the kitchens where she and Cook were doing the weekly baking.

"Ohhh! I cannot believe it! It is impossible! I must be dreaming!"

"What is it, miss? What is it?"

"London! I am to go to London! On the very next mail coach!" The girl let the letter fall to the floor, grabbed the maid by the hands, and began to sing and dance around the dark, crowded room.

Giggling, they fell in a heap on one of the beds, only to be brought sharply back to reality by a gruff voice intoning, "Have you lost your senses, gel? Dancing and singing in the dormitory?"

Freezing for a moment before scrambling to their feet, the maid and the schoolgirl bowed their heads and tugged their gowns into place. The frosty dame in starched black took a step into the room, the loose floorboards groaning in protest. With a wave of her hand, the intimidating matron dismissed the maid.

Then, looking down her beaklike nose, she said coldly, "So, you are going to London, Miss Wyndridge. How delightful. Pack your things. You leave on the afternoon mail coach."

"Thank you, Miss Lowery. I'll do that."

"And, Miss Wyndridge, do try to be prompt."

"Yes, Miss Lowery."

The headmistress turned on her heel and marched out of the room. Miss Angelica Wyndridge allowed herself the luxury of reading her letter of deliverance one more time before she pulled out a tattered portmanteau and packed her only other dress, her threadbare flannel nightgown, and her comb. She looked in the mirror at her reflection and smiled. She could see remnants of the girl of seventeen, the girl she had been before the deaths of her grandmother and father had forced her out of Society and back to the schoolroom.

Now that her new guardian had finally returned from the wars, she could once again become Miss Angelica Wyndridge, a young lady of consequence. And this time, not in the middle of the countryside, but in London!

She carefully lifted her chin, looking down her nose at the beauty in the mirror, and said, "You will take London by storm, Miss Wyndridge! By storm!"

Sir Garrett Wyndridge reached for his sword without thinking and leapt from his bed with a bloodcurdling battle cry.

"Aiee!" squealed the new footman as his tray of hot coffee went flying through the air.

"Argh!" yelped the valet as the scalding liquid hit his thigh.

"Bloody hell!" snapped Garrett, throwing down the candlestick he had grabbed in the absence of his sword and reaching for his dressing gown to cover his state of undress.

"Never sneak up on a soldier! You know better than that!" he growled at the shaking footman.

"I'm sorry, Major—I mean Sir Garrett, sir," said the young footman. "Are you all right, Mr. Anderson?"

"I will be," replied the fastidious Anderson, "if I can get this coffee stain out of my breeches."

"And what of your burned leg?" said Garrett, grinning at his valet's horrified expression.

The valet waved an airy hand to signify that any injury to his person could not compare to a ruined pair of breeches. With a sympathetic smile, Garrett turned back to the footman, who was mopping up the spill and retrieving the broken shards of china.

"Why don't you go and see to it there is hot coffee for me in the breakfast room? I am not accustomed to waking to a tray in bed."

"Very good, sir," said the footman with an awkward bow, revealing for the hundredth time his lack of experience.

The young man would have saluted had his hands been free. Garrett hoped he would settle in soon; the lad had been a real asset on the field of battle, but the work of footman seemed to be taxing his abilities.

"You should turn him off, Sir Garrett," advised the valet, his nose elevated.

"Given time and patience, James will be fine, Anderson," said Garrett, pulling on his unmentionables. The valet produced a pair of riding breeches, but Garrett waved them away. "I'll eat first. I'm famished. I do believe a night of debauchery is much more exhausting than a battle," he added, raking a hand through his dark curls before heading out the door.

Garrett shook his head as his valet's colorful vocabulary floated down the hall to his ears. For all that Anderson acted like a prissy superior to the other servants, he was only a few steps away from the stable himself. Still, he had a way with boots that made him indispensable to a gentleman.

"Good morning, slugabed," said a familiar voice as Garrett entered his breakfast parlor.

"Humph," said Garrett, ignoring his visitor and heaping his plate from the sideboard. When he had filled the plate and found his chair, he commented, "You're out early this morning, Ian."

"Had t' be. You know my sister has come to town. I think it's time to find bachelor lodgings. I can stand the brats, but my sister is a real tartar. I may have inherited the father's red hair, but m' sister got the temper," said the lanky gentleman, his pale blue eyes twinkling merrily.

"You know I would ask you to stay here, but I'm shortly going to be saddled with my own brood of feminine boarders."

"Ah, yes, your wards. Tell me, have you ever seen any of them?" asked Mr. Emery, leaning his chair back on two legs and reaching behind him for another scone.

"I used to see Angelica from time to time at family gatherings. But the others? Not in donkey's years. And then only the oldest girl, Mystique. The younger one wasn't there; she was only a baby. But Mystique must have been about nine when my father took me up to the races, and we ran into this cousin of my mother's. I suppose it was fortunate we did; I mean, as I recall, Lambert was quite impressed by my equestrian abilities." At his friend's raised brows, Garrett chuckled. "I told you about it. I was seventeen at the time, and the fellow who was supposed to ride his favorite horse had taken ill. My father volunteered me."

"And made your fortune," said Ian with a chuckle.

"You could say so. I won the race for Cousin Lambert; I suppose he's just returning the favor. According to his solicitor, when he turned up his toes there were no sons to inherit, and the property wasn't entailed. He had to do something with it. Fortunately, he thought of me."

"Why not your older brother?" asked Ian, slathering another scone with jam.

"Not related. Robert's only my half brother, remember? I'm related to Lambert through my mother."

"But Lambert did have these two daughters. I suppose he provided for them."

"Well, I . . . he must have. Stands to reason, doesn't it? And he couldn't very well expect a girl to take over the Lambert Racing Stables, could he? That would bring it to its knees in no time!" said Garrett.

"Still, the stables would have made a handsome dowry."

"True, and there they would be, fair game for any fortune hunter who could turn them up sweet with no one to look out for them. Besides, I'll settle something on each of the girls if Lambert didn't see to it himself. Don't worry about that."

"When do they arrive?"

"I'm not certain; I've sent letters to all of them. I have also written to my sister-in-law, asking her to come for the Season and take over the job of chaperon. She should be happy of the chance to escape her children. There are five of them now, all boys!"

"Five! My, my, your brother Robert was busy while we were away fighting old Nappy. What will you do if your sister-in-law won't accept the job?" asked Ian, smearing jam on yet another of Cook's tasty scones.

"Why, I . . . but she'll leap at the chance. My sister-in-law is a great gun! She won't fail me," said Garrett, taking a large bite of pigeon pie as he began opening the morning post.

"Ah, most satisfactory," he murmured as he read the brief letter from his cousin Angelica. He looked up and waved the letter toward his friend. "My cousin Angelica is delighted with my proposal, most appreciative of the opportunity for a Season in London. She says all that is appropriate."

"That's one down," said Ian.

"You know, Ian, aside from enjoying having my own home—two of them, as a matter of fact—I am discovering it is rather gratifying to be able to help out these girls. Take Angelica, for instance. She went to visit her grandmother in Bath two years ago when she turned seventeen, just to acquire a bit of polish before London, you know. Then her father died, her grandmother died, and with no one else to take her in, she found herself returned to the young ladies' seminary. What a setback that must have been!"

"Devil's own luck," commented Ian, slicing an apple into neat pieces. "So when does the angelic Angelica arrive?"

With a frown, Garrett returned to the letter. "Let's see . . . she arrives . . . today? But that can't be! I'm not ready! Caroline's not even here!"

"Well, you'll just have to put up in a hotel until Caroline gets here," said Ian Emery, wiping his mouth and then dusting the front of his waistcoat with long, slender fingers.

"I can't do that! I can't leave an innocent young girl alone in a house in London with no one but servants to look after her. I may not know much about the way the ton works, but I'm not a complete sapskull."

Ian snapped his fingers. "I have it! Send her to my sister's house and let her stay with them. I'll stay here with you until I can find a more permanent arrangement."

"That might do," said Garrett thoughtfully. "Very well, but I . . . Ah, here is the letter from Caroline. No doubt she has written to let me know when to expect her. That's better," said Garret, smiling again. The smile faded as he perused his sister-in-law's letter. With a snort of disgust, he threw it onto the table. "Women!"

"Problem?" asked his friend, barely suppressing his amusement.

"Caroline. She's not coming! Seems she's increasing, yet again, and can't risk traveling at this time. What the devil am I going to do?"

"Don't panic, old man. First, you need to look in the family Bible. Then—"

"Devil take you! I don't need religion! I need a chaperon!" snapped Garrett.

"Exactly, you dolt! And where does one find suitable chaperons? From the family, that's where! Somewhere in the family Bible there must be a list of all the females in the past generation. All you have to do is look through there, find one who's widowed or a spinster, someone who's not likely to have much money. Someone who'll be thankful for a roof over her head and a bit of light duty. Write back to Caroline if you can't think of anyone. She's bound to know of someone in the family!"

"Yes, yes, you're right. I remember my mother had two spinster aunts, cousins, something; they used to pinch my cheeks every time I saw them and remark about how I had grown. Until, of course, I patted one of them on her rather large stomach and told her she had grown, too. Got sent to bed without my supper, but it was worth it."

"Well, there you have it! Contact them, and they'll be here in a trice to help you out."

Happy to have this problem well on the way to being solved, Garrett sifted through the remainder of his letters and pulled out the one from Yorkshire.

"Ah, here's the one from the other cousins, the Lambert sisters."

His brow drew together, and his green eyes sparkled with indignation as he read the brief letter from his distant cousins. "Of all the arrogant . . ."

"Another problem?" inquired Ian, chuckling openly now. "What was it you were saying about how pleasant it is to be able to help your indigent relations?"

"Stubble it," growled Garrett. "Listen to this," he said and proceeded to read Felicity's letter.

"So it's thank you very much, but no thank you, is

it?" said Ian. "Well, at least that's two females you won't have to worry about."

"You think not? They live in Yorkshire, in the house on the property where Lambert Racing Stables is . . . the stables I now own. How the devil am I going to be able to take over properly if they're still in residence? What am I to do? Throw them out?"

"As tempting as that might seem, I don't suppose you can," said Ian. "Perhaps they didn't understand the invitation precisely. You did explain that you would be footing the entire bill for the Season?"

"Of course I did. I don't expect them to pay for anything. They're just being stubborn."

"Maybe one of them has already formed an attachment."

"Humph! They may have, but nothing can come of it without my permission. I am, after all, their guardian," said Garrett, crumbling the letter in his fist.

"True, true. I tell you what, Garrett. Why not send Putty after them?"

Garrett shook his head, dismissing the idea instantly. "Putty? You must be kidding. That giant would frighten them half to dea—"

"Exactly!" said Ian. "He wouldn't hurt a fly, but they won't know that. He looks mean, and he sounds mean with that gruff voice of his. They'll have their bags packed before nightfall."

"I'll do it!" said Garrett, slamming his palm down on the table. Then he grinned at his friend and said, "You know, Ian, you are quite a strategist."

"That's why Wellington found my advice indispensable," quipped his long-legged friend.

"Well, shall we say, sometimes acceptable?" said Garrett, grinning at his friend. "Now, the first thing we must do is talk your sister around to taking in Angelica."

"We? Oh, no, you're on your own with that one. If I say one word for it, you know Maggie will kick up a fuss. Much better if you go alone and plead your case. I always thought she fancied you. You can turn her up sweet."

"Coward," said Garrett, rising.

"Indubitably, at least where m' sister is concerned."

"You'd think you could charm her the way you do all the other ladies."

"Two points you're missing there, my friend. First of all, my sister knows me too well to fall for any of my flummery. Secondly, you're stretching it a bit by calling the females who do fall for my flummery ladies."

Ticking them off on his fingers, Garrett said, "And what of Miss Beauchamps? Or the widow Canfield? Or—"

"Very well, if you mean to be meticulous, then there are some ladies who are willing to fall victim to my charms."

"Face it, Ian; in the short time we've been home, you've earned the reputation of rake."

"Hardly."

"Oh, not a hardened rake, perhaps, but a man of some danger. That makes you all the more exciting to the ladies."

"The best thing about my reputation, my friend, is

that I am no longer plagued by pushy mamas trying to saddle me with their daughters."

"But what a price to pay," laughed Garrett.

"And what of you, Garrett? There is the matter of that little opera dancer in your keeping."

"Not in my keeping . . . not yet," said Garrett, his handsome facing breaking into a grin. "But let us forget about the ladies for the moment. It's a subject both of us should try to avoid as much as possible since we are shortly to be overrun. I propose we go to Gentleman Jackson's and work off a little of last night's carousing."

"A capital idea! You get dressed, and I'll have another scone."

"Good grief, Ian, how many have you had?"

"Only a half dozen or so."

"A normal man would have run to fat years ago eating the way you do."

"Isn't it lucky that I'm an extraordinary man?" quipped the redhead.

"Well, out of the ordinary, perhaps. I'll be down in twenty minutes."

"There's a man t' see you, Lady Miss," said the ancient butler, scowling his disapproval.

"What sort of man, McMann?" asked Missy Lambert, looking up impatiently from her father's scarred old desk which was littered with papers and ledgers.

"Naught but a servant; still and all, he's a giant of a man, miss. Says he's from London."

"What's his business? Is he looking to buy a horse? Find a sire for his mare?"

"He won't say, miss. Says as how yer th' only one he'll talk to," said the old man, scratching his balding pate. "He did say something about his commanding officer."

"I don't have time for such games, McMann. Send him away."

"I'll try," said the servant doubtfully. As he left the room, he muttered loudly enough for his mistress to hear, "If he wants t' be sent away."

Missy returned to the column she was totaling before the interruption, but her concentration had flown. In disgust, she threw down the pen and sat back, expelling a breath with unladylike force. Rising, she followed the butler to the main hall.

"I'll wait," growled a massive man, his face hidden by the glare of sunshine streaming through the open doorway behind him. He proceeded to back up against the wall, crossing his arms and tucking in his chin, his beady eyes peering straight ahead; his mouth clamped shut tightly, causing his jowls to spill over the collar of his coat.

A shiver of disquiet running up and down her spine, Missy stepped into the morning room, frowning fiercely. What was she to do? Other than McMann, there was only one footman in the house. They were hardly a match for the recalcitrant giant.

"Missy! Missy! I have had the most wonderful morning!" called Felicity, entering through the front door, her arms filled with packages.

Just as Missy stepped into the hall, their massive visitor shoved off of the wall, blocking her sister's progress. Her boxes stacked high, Felicity ran into the obstacle, bounced off, and sent packages flying.

"Oh!" she screamed, her eyes wide with fright as her gaze made a rapid ascent, traveling from belt to chest to chin. "Oh," she repeated, wilting to the floor.

Her head never touched the marble tiles. The giant swept her into his arms, elbowed past the butler and Missy, and gently placed Felicity on the sofa in the morning room. With a dexterity surprising in a man so large, he rose and swiveled around, spying the decanters. Pulling out a clean handkerchief, he poured a fine old sherry over the cloth and returned to Felicity's side, bathing her face and wrists with a gentle touch.

"Let me," said Missy, forgetting her initial fear of the servant and coming forward.

"Gently," commanded the giant.

"Oh, dear, how silly of me," said Felicity, coming to and quickly trying to rise.

"Just lie still, dear. You fainted," said her sister.

"I . . . I know. You must forgive me, Mr. . . . uh . . ." she said, holding out her hand to the giant.

"Putty; just Putty. I'm sorry I scared you," said the visitor, his bulldog face creasing into a shy smile.

"Not at all, Putty, I hope you'll forgive me for being so silly," said Felicity, sitting up slowly and swinging her feet to the floor. Everyone waited to make certain she would remain upright.

Felicity continued brightly, "I suppose it was the fatigue of my morning. I'm not usually so faint-hearted. I, uh, don't believe we've met before, have we?"

The servant shook his head, still smiling.

"Mr. Putty came to see me on business," said Missy, reinserting herself into the conversation. "McMann, fetch some refreshments for our guest and something restorative for my sister. Would you care to accompany me to my office, Putty?" she asked, pointing the way toward the door.

The giant shook his head and opened his coat, taking an envelope from the inner pocket of his jacket.

"I came to take you ladies to London," he pronounced gravely, favoring Missy with a lowered brow before turning back to Felicity with another smile.

"The devil you say," exclaimed Missy, flushing uncomfortably when the giant turned his startled gaze on her.

Felicity placed a light hand on Putty's sleeve and said, "I must apologize for my sister, Mr. Putty. She is not accustomed to following orders."

"Everyone has to follow orders," pronounced the giant.

Opening the envelope, Missy moved away from the group, her heart beating rapidly. She had known, of course, that the new heir would probably follow up his invitation with a demand. She had hoped, however, to have more time before it arrived. She hated confrontation, for all that she was accustomed to dealing with men and their tempers. Horses were so much easier. She knew what to expect from them, and after awhile they knew what to expect from her. All in all, horses were much pleasanter than people, she thought, giving Sir Garrett Wyndridge's letter a quick read.

He had lost his subtlety this time. This was not a

command performance couched in a charming invitation. No, this was an order, pure and simple. She grimaced, reread the letter again, and sighed.

Missy glanced toward her sister, who was now pouring out for their oversized caller. He was perched on the edge of the sofa, as far from Felicity as he could get, balancing a plate of biscuits on one big knee and sipping tea from a delicate porcelain cup. Missy would have laughed at the scene, but their case was too serious.

Pasting a smile on her face, she said brightly, "I suppose there is no help for it, Felicity. It seems we have been summoned to London, so to London we shall go! I do hope, Mr. Putty, you don't mind waiting until morning before we leave."

The giant sprang to his feet; Felicity caught the saucer before it hit the floor, but the biscuits rolled about like ninepins.

"Morning will be fine, Miss Lambert," said Putty, his color high. "If you don't mind putting me up in the barn?"

"I think we can do better than that," said Felicity. Turning to the butler, who hovered by the door, she said, "McMann, please show Mr. Putty to a room in the servants' hall."

"Very good, Miss Felicity."

When they were alone, Felicity turned to her sister, who had remained on the far side of the room gazing out the window, her head held proudly, the letter clutched tightly in her hand.

"It will be agreeable to see London, don't you think, Missy? Quite like an adventure."

"Quite," came the monosyllabic response.

"And we won't have to pinch pennies," Felicity added wistfully.

At this, Missy looked up with a smile. "No, you won't have to pinch pennies. I'm certain our guardian will be very generous. If he were not a generous man, he would never have offered to give you a Season."

"*Us* a Season," said Felicity gently. "And only think, you have always wanted to visit Tattersall's."

"Ladies can't go to Tattersall's, Felicity. You know that. That's just one of the things ladies aren't supposed to do."

"I know it will be difficult for you, Missy. I mean, you are accustomed to being in charge. I can hardly remember when you weren't in charge around here; Papa was ill for so long. But for once, you can relax and not have to work so hard. Someone will take care of you for a change," said Felicity, her delicate features full of sympathy and hope.

For her sister's sake, Missy smiled, and Felicity breathed a sigh of relief.

"Now, what made your morning so wonderful?" asked Missy.

"Oh, I almost forgot! Come and see the beautiful wool I bought to make a blanket for King's Shilling. I hope you'll like it. It's a beautiful green; I thought it would be perfect with his chestnut coat." Tripping lightly into the hall, Felicity retrieved several of the boxes from the table where McMann had stacked them neatly.

"It is beautiful," said Missy, stroking the soft, thick cloth. "But how ever—"

"Oh, don't worry. I didn't waste the housekeeping

budget. I finished Mrs. Abernathy's dress lace last night, and she paid me handsomely for it. I had also done some embroidery for Mrs. Denny, the landlady at the inn. Anyway, I know it was extravagant, but I couldn't resist the wool when Mrs. Abernathy showed it to me. I'm afraid I also splurged on myself; I know I shouldn't have, but she had some of that French soap. I simply couldn't resist. You know you like it every bit as much as I do," she added.

"You are going to spoil King's Shilling, and me," teased Missy, her eyes clouding over. She turned away and took a deep breath.

What kind of life had she made for her sister that Felicity had to do handwork in order to buy the luxuries of life? And what kind of young woman spent her carefully earned coins on wool for a racehorse's blanket?

"But I enjoy buying things for you. After all you have done for me? Why, there's no one who deserves it more, Missy. That's why I'm glad we're going to London. I know you'll miss the farm and the horses, but it will give you a chance to be pampered for once in your life, the way you have always pampered me."

Missy opened her mouth to protest, but her sister's blue eyes held such love, such excitement, she couldn't dispel that happiness. Instead, she smiled, gave her sister a quick hug, and said gruffly, "I've got a million things to do if we are to leave in the morning. I'm sure you do, too."

"Oh, you're right! I have to talk to Cook about the maids, pack my sewing basket, and . . ."

Missy stroked the soft wool once more before closing the box and setting it back on top of the others.

From what she had heard of London, Felicity would have no time for making horse blankets or lace or anything else when they arrived in London. There were far too many balls and picnics and other such frivolities.

There would be no rides through the countryside, no spur-of-the-moment races across the meadows. There would be no horses to train, no hay to cut . . . nothing.

With a sigh, Missy shook her head. She missed Yorkshire already. But she had things to do; she couldn't stand around daydreaming all morning.

She hurried up the stairs to change for a visit to the farm steward. Price would be amazed at her news. Having grown up together, they were more like brother and sister than employer and employee. He would doubtless tease her about dancing and beaux.

Missy changed to a riding habit for the short ride to Price's house. She glanced at her image; even as she sat at the desk, her hair had managed to slip its pins. She released it from the tight chignon. It fell in long, dark waves almost to her waist. Missy raked a comb through it; then, looking over her shoulder, she wound it on top of her head and studied the effect.

Absurd! she told herself, hastily twisting it into another severe knot at the nape of her neck. Nothing could change her from a plain miss to a beauty.

Felicity would shine in new, fashionable gowns. She would be the center of attention. Missy would look out of place, like a sparrow imitating a swan.

Not that it mattered. She had no intention of seeking a husband in London—or anywhere else, for that matter! She would go and enjoy watching Felicity, but she would not get caught up in the social whirl, no matter what this guardian might think.

Most of all, she would not allow this upstart guardian to rule her emotions. Perhaps she had conceded and agreed to go to London; it didn't necessarily follow that she meant to cooperate with all his schemes, as he would soon find out!

Two

"I refuse to remain for one more day in that woman's house!" declared the haughty beauty, her eyes snapping with fire.

"But, Angelica, it wouldn't be proper for us to reside together here without a chaperon. I've already explained that," said Garrett wearily. "Tell her, Ian. It just wouldn't be proper."

Ian Emery shrugged his shoulders and shook his head before heading for the door. "Sorry, old man. You're on your own with that one," he said. "She may have only been here a week, but that was an hour too much for me. Good luck."

"Oooh! And good riddance to the man!" yelled Angelica. "Do you know he had the temerity to tell me I should do as his sister said? I am not a child!"

"Which is exactly why we mustn't reside in this house together without the benefit of a proper chaperon. If I were married—"

"I don't see why not!" she interrupted tartly, plopping down on the sofa in the library. "You did very well when you squired me to the theater two nights ago. And last night to Lady Phipps's card party. Everyone knows you are merely my guardian. Surely there can be nothing improper about that!"

"Only think of your reputation. Some might think, Angelica, that I am too young to be a proper guardian. You wouldn't wish to spoil your chances before the Season is well under way. I must agree with Maggie, you shouldn't even have attended those activities until we have someone here as chaperon. You don't know what the old tabbies are like. They will say I am too young, and that's all that matters."

"Too young? But that is ridiculous, Cousin Garrett. Why, you must be thirty years old!" She delivered this denunciation with such obvious distaste that her guardian could feel only dismay at his elderly status.

The butler entered, peering about the room for a moment to locate his master with his myopic stare. Finally he said, "Sir Garrett, a person to see you."

"Not now, Turtle."

"But it is a lady, a Miss Dill. Or, to be more precise, a gentlewoman, sir. I think you should see her," he suggested, pulling back his head quickly as his gaze found the haughty Miss Wyndridge glaring at him from her place on the sofa.

"She must be my mother's spinster cousin. Send her in!" said Garrett, rubbing his hands gleefully. Turning back to Angelica, he said happily, "You may just get your wish after all, my dear. If this Miss Dill is all that I expect, she will be the perfect chaperon for you and my other cousins. You'll be able to move back from Mr. Emery's sister's house immediately."

"I warn you, Cousin Garrett, whether she is perfect or not, I intend to do so," said the golden-haired beauty.

"Miss Agatha Dill," announced Turtle.

"Miss Dill, do come in. It has been so very long since we last met. I am Garrett Wyndridge, and this is another cousin, Miss Angelica Wyndridge."

"How do you do, Sir Garrett? My, my, you have changed. I haven't seen you since you were a boy. The last time I spoke to your mother, rest her soul, she told me how very handsome you had grown, and I can see she didn't exaggerate! You have the Wyndridge eyes, I see. Such a pretty shade of green."

Garrett blinked in surprise. This was surely not the way a proper interview for a position was supposed to be conducted, but he smiled and seated the elderly lady. Perhaps, he reflected, it was because Miss Dill was some sort of relation to him. He wished his mother were still alive so she could explain the matter. Miss Dill certainly looked to be a proper chaperon, dressed in pale gray, her white hair piled on top of her hair in a simple style.

"And this young lady is to be one of my charges? Why, you are a beauty. We should have no trouble firing you off. More like, we will have trouble fending off your suitors," she added with a laugh.

"Thank you, Miss Dill," said Angelica, mollified by this praise.

"I only speak the truth, child. And please, do call me Dillie; everyone does."

"Thank you, Dillie," said Angelica, a smile curving her generous lips.

Garrett breathed a sigh of relief. He grinned at himself; he didn't realize how desperate he was to be rid of the responsibility of escorting his cousin Angelica about town. And he had thought fighting Napoleon was a challenge; just let Angelica get hold of the little Corsican. That intrepid Frenchman would flee without a backward look!

Garrett smiled, focusing on this newest addition to his household, realizing she had addressed some remark to him. He apologized for his inattention, but Miss Dill wagged a finger at him and chuckled.

"No need to apologize, my boy. I saw you staring at Miss Angelica, Garrett. I don't have to be told twice how things are," she added with a broad wink.

"No!" said Garrett and Angelica, in perfect harmony for once.

"That is, my cousin is a lovely young woman, but I—"

"I would never choose someone so old, Dillie. Never!" Angelica struck a dramatic pose, the back of her hand to her brow, her eyes closed.

"Very well, if you insist," said Miss Dill, smiling still.

Garrett felt a twinge of unease; if Miss Dill insisted on playing the matchmaker, his life could become even more complicated.

He relaxed as the lady added affably, "I'm sure you both know your own minds. And you, Angelica, should have no trouble attracting any number of eligible parties. But I thought there were to be three of you. Where are my other charges?"

As if on cue, the door opened, and Turtle announced quickly, "The Misses Lambert, sir."

Garrett rose, sketching a brief bow before looking up at the bluest eyes he had ever seen. It took a moment to move beyond those incredible eyes and take in the face and expression. When he did, he took a step back as the unbridled hostility of those pursed lips registered with his mind.

"Miss Mystique Lambert?" he inquired, schooling his tone to one of polite coolness as he gazed from one young lady to the next. The second young lady's sweet expression was in sharp contrast, and he could tell immediately that she was the beauty of the family, though her blue eyes, like watercolors, were less intense than her sister's.

"I prefer Missy Lambert," said the hostile one.

"And I am Felicity Lambert. You must be Sir Garrett Wyndridge," said the beauty, stepping past her sister and extending a friendly hand.

Garrett reacted to the gesture automatically, his own smile, the smile that always had such a powerful effect on women, drawing her into the room warmly. It did not, however, appear to have any effect on Missy Lambert. Ignoring his hand, the petite young woman glanced around the drawing room, her gaze appraising, coming to rest on him briefly before she fixed those beautiful eyes on a spot somewhere beyond his left ear.

He cleared his throat awkwardly and said, "Please, call me Garrett, or Cousin Garrett if you wish. I am delighted to meet you, Felicity. I have met your sister before, of course, but you were just a baby and hadn't come to the races with your father."

"Oh, I never attended the races. I must confess horses rather frighten me," she replied, including everyone in her pleasant gaze. "Missy, of course, would live in the barn if she could," she added, favoring her sister with an affectionate smile.

"This is Miss Agatha Dill, who has come to us to

help you ladies navigate the waters of the Season successfully," said Garrett.

"How do you do?" said the reserved Miss Lambert.

"Very well, thank you. Missy, is it? I hope you don't
mind if I call you by your Christian name. If we are
to be family, I think it's best to begin the way we mean
to go on, don't you? And you must call me Dillie;
everyone does."

The newest arrivals nodded, and Garrett turned to
his other ward, who was beginning to fume at being
left to last.

"This is my other ward, Angelica Wyndridge. I believe you are also related to her in some distant manner," he added.

"Oh, yes; I think our grandmother and your father
were cousins on the Wyndridge side," said Felicity.

Angelica stifled a bored yawn, saying, "I have never
paid much attention to such distant connections."

Felicity blinked twice and turned to her sister, pulling her forward into the group.

Missy fixed Angelica with a hard stare, lifted her
strong chin, and declared, "Isn't it lucky for you that
Cousin Garrett does not endorse such self-suffi-
ciency."

Silence reigned for a few uncomfortable seconds
before Garrett cleared his throat, and Miss Dill announced, "Ah, the tea tray. I declare, I am famished,
and I am certain you young ladies must be also."

"No," said Missy.

"Oh, yes," said Felicity before looking at her sister
and saying, "That is, I'm sure we would prefer to
wash the dust of the road off before we join you."

"You may join them, if you wish, Felicity. I think I shall simply rest this afternoon."

"Yes, of course, Missy. That is what I was going to say," agreed Felicity.

Garrett opened his mouth to protest, but the cold, raised brow directed his way silenced him. He looked back at Felicity's pleading grimace and shrugged, saying, "Very well; I'll have Turtle take you to your rooms. I have given all of you ladies rooms in the west wing, if that is all right. Unless, of course, you are accustomed to some other rooms."

"No, Papa never brought us to London," said Felicity. "As a matter of fact, I don't remember his ever coming either. So any rooms will do, Cousin Garrett."

"Good. I shall have a tray sent up."

"That is not necessary," said the prune.

"Very well, if that is what you wish," replied Garrett, the muscle in his jaw beginning to stiffen.

"You may send me a tray, Cousin Garrett," said the delicate Felicity, her smile melting his ire slightly.

Then he turned and said, "Miss Dill—"

"That's Dillie, my boy. You must all call me Dillie," said the older woman.

"I forgot," replied Garrett, favoring her with a smile. "If you would care to go also. I know you only journeyed here from Islington, but if you wish to rest in your room, I will have a tray sent up."

"Nonsense, my boy, I am not so frail! Besides, I cannot bear the thought of leaving this delicious repast. Pour out, please, Angelica. Oh, very prettily done," she added.

"Come along, Felicity," said Missy, dragging her sister from the room before she could sink into a polite curtsey.

"We dine at eight o'clock, ladies. If you should require anything, you need only pull the bell rope. I have assigned a maid for you to share."

"Thank you," replied Felicity as Missy pulled her from the room.

"How rude," pronounced Angelica haughtily.

"Indeed it was," said Garrett, staring pointedly at his spoiled cousin.

She flushed uncomfortably and returned her attention to the food on her plate, ignoring his allusion to her own behavior.

When Garrett had finished his tea, he excused himself and went to the stables in search of Putty. He found the giant playing with the new kittens, his ham-sized hands gently stroking the soft fur with a tenderness Garrett could only marvel at. Putty started to come to attention when he saw his former officer, but Garrett waved him back, seating himself on a small stool and scooping up a tiny black kitten in his hands.

"How was the journey with the Misses Lambert, Putty?"

"Fine, sir. That Miss Felicity is as nice as can be," said the gentle giant.

"And Mystique Lambert? What do you make of her?" asked Garrett.

"She's all right, I suppose, but she's not as sweet as Miss Felicity."

"No, I can already tell that," said Garrett, shaking his head. "What was the estate like? Did it appear to be in order?"

"It was real pretty, sir. Lots of green grass and horses. 'Course, I stayed in th' house, not in th' barn like I'm used to. Miss Felicity saw to that; she said, as how it was so much colder up there than in London, I might take a cold if I slept in the barn. She made sure I had a soft bed and plenty of food," said Putty.

"Did you see much of the farm, the horses?"

"No, not really. There was one stallion Miss Lambert was working with the morning we left. I asked Miss Felicity about him, but she said he was her sister's pet."

Garrett placed the kitten back on the ground and stood up. "Humph, a stallion for a pet. A most unusual young lady, my cousin Mystique."

"I think you should call her something else, sir. She didn't seem to care for that name. She like to 'ave taken my head off when I first met her."

"I'll try and remember that, Putty. While they are in town, I wonder if you would mind being their groom. They may be full grown, but they are from the country and not used to London's ways. I wouldn't worry about them if I knew you were looking out for them."

The giant brightened, then frowned. "What about Miss Wyndridge?"

"No, I'll set someone else to look after her, unless they all go out together."

Nodding, Putty stood up, his stance almost at attention. "I'll make sure nothing happens to them, Major, sir."

"Good, thank you."

* * *

"Why could we not have gone back down for tea?" asked Felicity, her voice verging on the petulant, a sure sign she was feeling pulled, for she was never contrary.

Missy, who was staring out the window, ignored the question for a moment as she watched her guardian striding across the yard and through the small garden, disappearing as he entered the house again. Her jaw set, she turned back to her sister, who had removed her gown and put on a lacy wrapper. Missy's smooth brow was creased with a frown.

"I'm sorry, Felicity. Certainly, if that is what you wish, do go down and join Miss High and Mighty for tea. I would not give her or our guardian the satisfaction!"

"Very well, but I must have something, Missy. You know I cannot go for hours on end without something to eat. I am not like you. I should probably faint," said Felicity, pulling the bell rope. "We cannot all be as hardy as you are," she added, slipping back into the plush chair beside the fireplace.

Missy chuckled. "Pray do not try to play off your airs on me. I know how perfectly healthy you are, and how terribly healthy your appetite is. You may try to fool the gentlemen that you are some frail, weak damsel. I know better."

Missy strode to the door and opened it to the waiting maid. "Bring us some tea, please, and something to eat."

"Something substantial, please," called Felicity.

"What would you like, miss?"

Felicity hopped lightly to her feet and joined them at the door. "Some cheese and bread. And some scones and jam, if you have any. Really, just anything you can lay your hand to. We are famished."

"Very good, miss," said the maid, giving a quick curtsy before she hurried away.

Missy closed the door and grinned at her sister. "She will be telling them all downstairs that we are a couple of gluttons, you know."

"What do you care, Missy? You don't care what anyone in London thinks of you; at least, that is what you told me."

"And so I don't," she said proudly, turning away and walking toward the door that led to her adjoining room. She paused before disappearing and said, "Just make sure you call me when the tray arrives, not after you have had your way with it, young lady."

Missy looked around the comfortable chamber with its soft bed and inviting chairs by the fire. On the far side of the room was an escritoire beside the door that led to her dressing room. As in Felicity's room, there were windows overlooking the garden; they were open, and the late afternoon breeze carried with it the fragrance of roses, reminding her of spring and home.

Missy shook her head. Almost, she could forget that she had been summoned from her home by her high-handed guardian's whim. But not quite, she resolved, setting her thoughts firmly on the injustice of his wishes.

No, she would not fall so easily into this lap of luxury. She would not allow herself to be deluded by a handsome face. He was naught but a man, like so many before.

If there was one thing Missy knew about, it was

men. Her father's household had seen a constant parade of men, men desperate for money, desperate for the thrill of gambling on the winner of a race. They had taught Missy one thing: She would not be seduced by their flowery words, their promises.

Why, even her father had betrayed her, giving her birthright over to the care of a virtual stranger. More than that, he had given *her* over to the interloper, her guardian, until the age of five and twenty! Two more years. Until then, she would have to be strong and wary.

But for now, she thought, yawning and stretching, sleep. *You must have sleep,* she told herself, sinking onto the feather mattress.

She didn't mind that her dreams were clouded with images of a smiling man with dark, curly hair and wonderful green eyes; she never remembered her dreams.

"Missy! Didn't you hear the dressing bell? We'll be late!" said Felicity, hurrying through the room and into the next, returning immediately with a silk gown of deep blue. "Wake up! Oh, do get on your feet, sister!"

Moaning, Missy did as she was told, standing obediently and allowing her sister to prod and pull at her until she was fully awake and practically dressed.

"What happened to tea?" she asked as her stomach let loose a great growl.

"I tried to wake you, but you were sleeping too soundly," said Felicity, pulling the remaining pins from Missy's hair and setting it free. It sprang forth in a riot of thick waves, framing her face.

"Ouch! That hurts!" she protested as her sister raked a comb through the long tresses. "Here, let me," she added crossly, taking the comb from her sister.

"There's the bell for dinner, Missy. I do hope Cousin Garrett doesn't lose his temper over our being a little late."

A strange light came into Missy's blue eyes, and she smiled. *Just let him lose his temper,* she thought, slowly twisting her hair into a tight chignon at the nape of her neck. She began securing it with the pins.

"Do you think Cousin Garrett will allow us to go shopping tomorrow?" asked Felicity.

"I suppose we might, if Sir Garrett was serious about that bit of his invitation," said Missy. "Of course, he may have changed his mind. The cost of dressing three women for a Season must be enormous!"

"Oh, surely he wouldn't be so dishonorable!"

Missy relented; though she was skeptical of her new guardian's intentions, she couldn't bear to see her sweet sister so upset.

"Of course not," said Missy. "I've just got a case of the grumbles. You know how I am when I first get up. Now, let me find my slippers."

"It seemed like such a good idea when I started on this insane scheme," said Garrett, running distracted fingers through his dark hair.

"That was before you met the divine and terrifying

Angelica Whine-ridge," said Ian Emery before taking a long pull on his claret. "She would be enough to deter the most desperate fortune hunter. Quite put me off my feed, and I had no intention of pursuing her."

"I should say not. At least I don't have to worry about that," said Garrett.

"I say, Garrett, is that any way to speak of your oldest friend? If the girl didn't absolutely frighten me to death, I would be quite cut up by your lack of faith in me."

"Rubbish! You know very well you are not the sort a guardian looks for in a suitor for his ward. You have enjoyed far too much success with women. By the way, how is the exquisite Lady Esther?"

"Doing very well, if you must know, but we have wandered from the point," said Ian. "If you are not worried about Angelica, then what? I refuse to believe that the other two could be as bad as Angelica."

"Oh, I grant you Angelica is a bit daunting, Ian, but she is not the worst of it. The one that has me most perplexed is Mystique . . . I mean, Missy."

"An antidote, is she? Still, you mean to settle a large enough dowry on the girl. Someone will take her off your hands, if only for the money," said the rake. "Thank heavens it won't have to be me. I don't think I could swallow a wife with some off-putting deformity, not even with a lively mistress to help me forget about her from time to time."

"Don't be a dolt, Ian. The girl doesn't have a deformity! She's a rare beauty, if you must know . . ."

"Ah, now I am intrigued," said Ian, straightening

his lanky legs and rising. "She must be an incomparable to merit praise from the gloomy Sir Garrett."

"She would be if she had any manners. But perhaps I'm being too harsh on the girl. After all, they had been on the road for several days. Perhaps she was just weary when we met this afternoon."

"Even finding excuses for her. I'm all agog to meet this country cousin."

"Good, because I put you between her and Miss Dill."

"The old one? Now, is that any way to treat a friend?" asked Ian.

"Very well. I'll exchange Miss Dill for Angelica," said Garrett, giving Ian a devilish grin.

Ian held up his hands as if to ward off such an occurrence. The dinner bell rang, and they left Garrett's cozy study and made their way toward the dining room.

Garrett frowned when they arrived and found only Miss Dill and Angelica waiting for them. They waited for a moment before Garrett offered his arm to Dillie and led the way into the room.

After several moments, Garrett nodded to the butler and announced, "We shan't wait any longer. I daresay my cousins were too worn out to join us."

The door swung open, and Missy entered. She was dressed in sapphire silk, an ancient gown Felicity had found in the attics at home and had cleverly altered to a more current fashion.

Caught off guard by the rush of heat Missy's entrance had engendered, Garrett stole a glance at his friend to gauge his reaction. Ian's bored gaze had dropped to his waistcoat where he plucked at a loose thread. Garrett breathed a sigh of relief. "Come in, ladies. We were afraid the journey had taken its toll and you had decided against joining us this evening," he said, smiling while he ignored the tiny trickle of perspiration that wended its way down his temple. He would have to speak to Turtle about making the fires smaller.

"We are not such frail creatures," said Missy coldly, effectively chilling the heat on Garrett's brow.

"Indeed we are not, Cousin Garrett," said Felicity, stepping into the room.

Garrett heard Ian's swift intake of breath and turned, diverted. His friend had straightened in his chair, leaning forward slightly as he stared, his eyes unwavering as he watched Garrett's youngest ward. One hand flew to his cravat to tug it into place; the other swept nervously through his red hair.

"Missy and Felicity Lambert, may I present my good friend Ian Emery? Ian, these are my wards, Miss Lambert and Miss Felicity."

Ian leapt to his feet, almost knocking over his chair in his effort to reach Felicity's chair before the footman could pull it out for her. With a bemused expression on her face, Missy found her own place beside Mr. Emery's.

"Thank you, Mr. Emery," said Felicity, favoring him with her sweet smile.

"My pleasure, Miss Felicity," said Ian. Suddenly he looked around, realized the spectacle he was making of himself, and returned to his chair, opposite Felicity.

The footmen, under the direction of the butler Turtle, began to serve the first course. It being such a small gathering, conversation was general so no one noticed Ian's lack of participation at first.

"Mr. Emery, how is it you know my cousin?" asked Missy for the second time.

"What? Oh, forever," said Ian, sparing Missy only the briefest of glances.

"Really," said Missy coolly. "But how did you meet? Were you at school together?"

It was obvious that this depth of conversation was putting a strain on Ian's concentration, but he finally replied, "Yes, at school, in the army, everything."

"I see," said Missy, her blue eyes dancing as she studied Ian Emery studying her sister.

Felicity had been having the same effect on males since she turned fifteen. With a wicked smile, Missy produced yet another question to torment her dinner partner.

Garrett, who had observed this exchange, tried to distract his cousin with a bluff, "Yes, Ian saved my life countless times."

"Oh, do tell," said Felicity, looking from one gentleman to the next with every evidence of interest.

Garrett had to admit she was a charming child, both pretty and genial, effortlessly putting at ease everyone within her range. Unfortunately, her elder sister did not possess the same talent.

With a smile, Garrett leaned forward, saying confidentially, "There was this one time . . . but perhaps you ladies . . ." Garrett grinned at the chorus of protests. Only his cousin Missy didn't seem eager to hear his story, he thought. Nevertheless, he continued. "There was the most horrible tyrant; everyone was terrified of the man. I shudder to think—"

"One of your commanding officers?" asked Felicity, her wide-eyed expression flitting from one man to the other.

"Worse than that!" declared Garrett grimly. "He was the headmaster at school!"

"Oh, not this one, Garrett," said Ian, who was quickly hushed by the ladies.

Garrett leaned forward and whispered, "We called him Ghastly Griffin."

The ladies giggled their appreciation of his histrionics. He looked past Angelica to Missy; she allowed only a tiny glimmer of amusement to show in her eyes before returning her attention to her food.

"Well, the headmaster was well known for his love of drink. Someone dared me to substitute vinegar for his wine one evening," said Garrett.

"How childish," said Angelica.

"I should hope so. I was all of twelve at the time," said Garrett. "Anyway, I managed the switch, but when he tasted it, and spewed it all over the table, I might add, he was beside himself with fury. He ranted and raved, refusing to allow anyone to leave until the culprit came forward."

"It was very bad of you, Cousin Garrett," said Felicity before adding eagerly, "But what did you do?"

"Do? Why, I did nothing; I was too terrified. Ian here confessed to the whole. When I tried to confess too, Ghastly Griffin punished both of us."

"That was unfair!" said Dillie.

"Ghastly Griffin wasn't known for fairness," said Ian, "and Garrett is only telling part of the story. I'm the one who challenged him in the first place."

"Were you? I had forgotten about that part of it,"

lied Garrett, grinning at each lady in turn, his gaze falling on Missy last and resting there.

As if she could feel his gaze on her, she raised her chin, her blue eyes meeting his evenly. One brow quirked upward, in challenge. Then she dropped her gaze again, and Garrett expelled the breath he didn't even realize he had been holding in.

"What the deuce," he muttered under his breath.

"So, what do you think of my new wards?" asked Garrett when the ladies had adjourned to the drawing room, leaving him and Ian to their port.

"Charming; utterly charming. Not at all like the other one," said Ian dreamily.

"Both of them?" asked Garrett.

"What? Oh, yes, both of them. The younger one is more personable, I think, but they are both quite lovely. The elder one is a bit too short to be in fashion, but she has a decent sort of figure. You shouldn't have any trouble getting her off your hands. I don't know what you were worried about. As for the other one, Felicity . . . she's a diamond of the first water. You'll have to keep an eye on her."

Garrett appeared to be concentrating on lighting his cigar, but he watched Ian covertly between the puffs of smoke.

"You don't think . . . that is, she's not your type," he stated carefully.

"My type?" said Ian Emery, shaking his head for emphasis. "No; too young, too naive for me. Need to find a nice young chap for Miss Felicity, not some cynical old rake like me." He met his friend's level gaze without flinching.

Garrett shrugged; Ian was an excellent card player for the very fact that he could lie so convincingly. But he seemed sincere in his protests. Garrett relaxed. It would never do for Ian and his innocent little ward to form a tendre for each other. They were totally unsuited.

"What about the other one? What did you think of Missy?"

"A bit too cold for me," said Ian. "I daresay she will improve with acquaintance."

"I suppose so. I can't help but feel she is out of charity with me, but for the life of me, I cannot figure out why. Haven't I done everything a good guardian is supposed to do? Haven't I given both her and her sister the opportunity for a Season so they may find suitable husbands? Yet I have caught her on several occasions looking daggers at me. It's enough to put a fellow off his feed."

"I know just what you mean; just the sort of thing my sister tries to do with me," said Ian. "But you may be wrong. Why don't we join the ladies, and you can find out?"

"Capital idea. Let's join the ladies," agreed Garrett.

Before they reached the drawing-room doors, they could hear the music, a sweet voice accompanied by rolling arpeggios on the pianoforte. Stepping forward eagerly, Garrett paused on the threshold. The clear voice originated, as he had guessed, from Felicity. At the pianoforte sat the intriguing Mystique Lambert, a tear rolling slowly down her cheek as she lost herself in the hauntingly beautiful melody.

The music ended. Ian stepped forward to take Felicity's hand and escort her to her seat. Missy remained at the pianoforte, her proud profile outlined by candlelight. She couldn't be over five foot three, but she looked positively regal in that pose, thought Garrett.

Suddenly she looked up and caught sight of him. She ducked her head, swiping at the emotional tears surreptitiously.

Then she rose and excused herself to the others. Walking calmly to the door and past him, she bade him a soft, "Good night," and was gone.

Garrett could not prevent himself from turning to watch her stately ascent of the stairs until she was out of sight.

Ian had said her looks were merely ordinary. Ordinary? Missy Lambert? Never!

Three

Missy stretched and yawned, opening her eyes and blinking several times before she recalled her situation. Somehow she had expected London to be noisier than this. She climbed out of bed and padded across to the window, throwing it open to the morning chill. It was a sunny day; the fragrance of the roses once again drifted up to her nostrils. Somewhere she heard a horse whinny. Smiling, she crossed to the dressing room, selected her favorite riding habit, a dull gold affair with black braid, and began divesting herself of her nightrail. It never occurred to her that a proper young lady would have summoned her maid.

When Missy reached the small stable, she paused and breathed deeply, the odors of straw and manure, horses and polished leather wrapping around her like an old friend. She strolled along the brick-lined aisle, sizing up the horses in the stalls. She had always found that the cattle a man kept spoke volumes about his character. Her guardian's horses were not showy, though the pair of matched grays appeared powerful. They all looked to be in fine health, and their stalls were covered in fresh straw, a sure sign of a careful master.

"Good morning, Miss Lambert," said the giant Putty, tugging on his cap in salute.

"Good morning, Mr. Putty. I wish to go for a ride," she announced. "Which mount would you suggest?"

He scratched his head for a moment before shaking it sadly.

"I don't think th' major thought about you ladies needing horses. Leastwise, he hasn't bought any ladies' hacks yet."

How shabby of Sir Garrett! Surely the man knew they would want to ride. Not that she would have submitted to being mounted on such a tame beast as a "ladies' hack."

Missy reined in her irritation at this news and said rationally, "Then which horse is accustomed to the saddle?" When Putty appeared puzzled by this, she expounded on her request. "I mean, which horses does Sir Garrett ride rather than hitch up to a carriage?"

"Oh! Th' major keeps two hacks. There's Tucker and Horse."

"Imaginative names," muttered Missy before commanding, "Show them to me, if you please."

Putty led her to the last two stalls. Inside the first was a fine gelding, coal black and at least sixteen hands. Next was a mare, of the Godolphin line, Missy judged by the shape of her head and her size.

"Which is this one?" she asked, pointing to the mare.

"That's Tucker, miss."

"She'll do. Saddle her, please."

Putty shifted nervously from one foot to the other, but still he did not enter the stall. Growing impatient, Missy raised her eyes past his barreled chest; his mouth was working as if to speak, but no sound was forthcoming.

"If you are not allowed to do so, show me where her tack is, and I will saddle her myself. I am quite capable, you know."

When he still made no move, Missy threw up her hands in disgust and stalked back down the row to the open tack room. The polished bridles and harnesses hung in neat rows, each labeled with its owner's name. She picked up the bridle for Tucker and looped it over one arm. Then, taking the saddle below it, she returned to the stall.

As she opened the door, Putty came to life. "Miss, please, miss. I don't think you should be doing that. Th' major's going to have my hide! Please, miss. Come out of there."

By this time, Missy had the bridle buckled into place and had thrown the saddle across the mare's back. As she leaned down to grab the cinch, she said, "If you wish to accompany me, Mr. Putty, I suggest you go and saddle your own hack."

"That won't be necessary, Putty. I will accompany Miss Lambert this morning," said Garrett, dismissing the relieved groom with a wave of his hand.

He watched approvingly as Missy expertly secured the saddle, leaning heavily against the mare's bloated side to make her expel that last breath so she could give the cinch one final pull.

"Do you always go about taking other people's horses without so much as a by your leave?" Garrett asked conversationally. "For all you know, the mare could be a real rotter."

Missy turned; her eyes narrowed. "If you had bothered to equip your stable with mounts suitable for a lady, I would not have been forced to appropriate your personal mount."

"Touché," said Garrett. "If you will be patient for a moment, Missy, I'll saddle Horse and join you."

When Garrett led his gelding from the stall, Missy was already mounted. He would have complimented her on her seat, but the tension still crackled between them. Privately, he had to admit she looked magnificent on horseback. Tucker was a neat bay, and Missy's habit was a dull gold; they made a handsome pair.

Garrett led the way out of the stable yard and into Portman Square. Neither spoke until they had threaded their way through the busy streets to Hyde Park.

Ever one for honesty, Missy said grudgingly, "Thank you for coming with me. I might well have taken a wrong turn without you."

"You're welcome. I should warn you, perhaps, that Tucker has a tendency to bolt for home if you don't keep an even tension on the reins at all times. Hence her name," said Garrett.

"Tucker? Why, she's as docile as a lamb."

"Most of the time, but you can't let up. First she balks, then she'll tuck her tail like a dog and before you know it, she's taken the bit between her teeth and is running flat out. She doesn't care who or what gets in the way."

"Thank you, Sir Garrett. I'll remember that," said

Missy, smiling at him as she kicked her heels and sent Tucker trotting ahead of him.

Garrett frowned. Did she have to be so demmed formal? And why did he feel she was enjoying some private joke at his expense? He looked down to make sure he hadn't popped a button or something. When he looked up, his ward was almost out of sight down the path. Grumbling, he sent the long-legged Horse after her at a swift canter.

By the time Garrett had caught her up, he had his temper well in hand. Still, he felt compelled to enlighten his ward on a thing or two.

"You ride very well, but there are a few things you should know about riding in London. First of all, you must always have a groom in attendance if I am unavailable. Having your sister or Angelica with you is not enough. Furthermore, if a gentleman invites you for a drive, you cannot go in a closed carriage, only something open, like a curricle."

Missy's eyes flashed blue ice, and she snapped, "First of all, I do not need an explanation as to what constitutes an open carriage, Sir Garrett. Secondly, I am not accustomed to being told what to do. I have been my own mistress for some time, sirrah."

"But that was at home. This is London; the rules have changed," said Garrett, pulling up and looking her in the eye without flinching.

"Your rules!" she spat.

"No, Society's rules. And while you may have no care for your own reputation, I'll not have the reputations of your sister and cousin ruined just because you wish to take the bit between your teeth!" retorted

Garrett, turning his mount and maneuvering him so he could be face to face with Missy.

"Is that understood, Mystique?" he asked with deadly calm.

Missy lifted her hand to slap his smug face. Tucker saw her chance, tucked her tail, grabbed the bit with a shake of her head, and took off. Missy was too experienced a horsewoman to scream; instead she cooed soothingly to the mare as she sawed feverishly on the reins. When she saw the park gates approaching, all she could think of were the wagons and coaches and carts they had passed on their sedate journey to the park. Panic welled up in her breast, seeking to spew forth. Then a strong hand snaked out, grabbing the bridle just beside Tucker's mouth, twisting the mare's head to the side. Missy held on tight as the mare's gait came to a plunging halt.

She gulped down a mouthful of air, then another.

"Are you all right?" asked Garrett, his expression stormy rather than concerned. Missy nodded. "I told you to keep an even tension on the reins. You might have been killed in the streets. And Tucker might have been maimed."

"Well, we weren't," snapped Missy, tears welling in her blue eyes. With head held high and an even tension on the reins, she led the way out of the park, trying to ignore the presence of her insufferable guardian.

She had never been so mortified. Of all the times for her to lose control of her horse! And then to compound her folly by crying!

When they reached the stable yard, Missy slipped to the ground and gladly turned the reins over to

Putty. She hurried toward the house, happy to be rid of Garrett and the dreadful knowledge that if she had been paying attention to the mare instead of her guardian, the mare would never have been able to run away with her.

Run away with her! She groaned inwardly for the hundredth time. She hadn't had that happen in years! Why did it have to happen with her guardian watching? How lowering!

"Missy, a moment, please," said Garrett, touching her sleeve.

Her arm began to tingle, and Missy felt a bizarre flash of heat travel upward; she felt sure she was blushing, but Garrett didn't appear to notice. He pointed toward a stone bench almost hidden by a rose-covered arbor. Seated beside her, he bowed his head for a moment to collect his thoughts.

"Missy, I'm sorry you are not happy about having to come to London. Putty told me you were less than pleased to leave Lambert Stables." He paused, giving her the opportunity to speak, but she only stared at her hands that were nervously pleating and unpleating the skirt of her habit.

"I understand your reluctance to leave home, but surely you can set aside your feelings and enjoy this Season. Your sister seems willing to throw herself into the fray, so to speak," he added, grinning at her profile.

Missy turned those blue eyes on him and nodded. "It is because of my sister that I have come to London. Without me, I don't think Felicity would have come, and I want her to have the opportunity to enjoy herself, to meet other young ladies her age, and perhaps to find a husband."

Garrett smiled at her, and this time he was gratified to see that his cousin was not completely immune to his smile. A teasing light in his eyes, he asked, "And what of you, Missy? You are hardly in your dotage. Surely you can find something or even someone in all of London to amuse you."

"It is said that nothing is impossible, Sir Garrett, but I have no such expectations. It is enough that Felicity should have a successful Season," said Missy.

"I see."

"Is that all?" she asked, rising.

"One more thing, Missy. Why do you persist in calling me Sir Garrett when your sister calls me Cousin Garrett?"

Missy chuckled, a sound that made Garrett lean toward her, hoping to hear more.

"When you can figure out in what way we are cousins, I will call you cousin. The relationship, if it truly exists, is so tenuous I don't feel comfortable claiming it."

Garrett laughed along with her. Then he said, "In truth, I have no idea how we are related. I suppose my mother, if she were still alive, could explain it. But, Missy, perhaps for the sake of Society, it would be best if you called me Cousin Garrett?"

She cocked her head to one side before nodding. "Very well, I will, so long as we are in company."

"Thank you."

"Good day, Cousin Garrett. Felicity and Angelica have made plans to go to the modiste today, so I daresay I shan't see you again until dinner."

* * *

Missy felt weary as she climbed the stairs, seeking the security of her chamber. Odd, she thought, to feel exhausted after a morning ride. As a rule, she felt invigorated when she returned from one.

Stripping off her habit, she gazed at the small selection of gowns she had brought to London. Nothing appealed to her at the moment, and she slipped back into her comfortable wrapper. She pulled the bell rope to order toast and chocolate in her room rather than going downstairs.

Coward, whispered a little voice in her head, but she frowned it away. After stirring the meager flames in the fireplace, she curled up in the comfortable cherry-striped chair to wait for the maid.

"Missy? Are you awake?" mumbled Felicity as she stumbled in through the door to her adjoining room.

"Of course, pet. Come in and join me. I'm sure Dulcie here can find another cup for us," she said, making her statement a request to the shy maid who curtsyed and nodded, hurrying from the room.

With an affectionate smile, Missy gave her cup of steaming chocolate to Felicity, who had slumped into the matching chair across from her.

"You are the only person I know who can still look pretty when your hair is coming down about your ears and you are half asleep," said Missy, her comment earning her a small smile. "What are the plans for today?"

"We are going shopping, of course. Angelica says until we have suitable wardrobes, we cannot hope to cut a dash in Society," said Felicity, her sparkle returning as she spoke.

"And just what does Angelica consider a suitable wardrobe?" asked Missy.

"We must have ball gowns, carriage dresses, morning dresses, afternoon gowns, and riding habits. Then there are all the accoutrements to go with them: the bonnets, gloves, shawls, unmentionables, and shoes," said the younger woman, her excitement growing. "I can hardly wait!"

"Now, Felicity, you don't wish to bankrupt Cousin Garrett," said the ever cautious Missy.

Felicity's face fell, and she said anxiously, "Oh, you do not think we could, do you? I had thought, since he reassured us again last night, that he could well afford the cost. But I'm sure you are right; I promise not to be too extravagant."

Missy felt a pang of conscience. Certainly she didn't like Sir Garrett being thrust on her as a guardian, but he was providing her dear sister with all that she couldn't. Because of his generosity, Felicity would have her Season, her opportunity to shine. She deserved it; she had spent her entire life making do and had never complained.

Tears sprang to Missy's eyes, and she threw her arms around her sister and hugged her neck, almost upsetting the cup of chocolate.

Bemused, Felicity set down the cup and asked, "What was that for, Missy?"

"Nothing!" said Missy brightly, springing to her feet and pulling her sister up also. "Come on. Let's get dressed and go downstairs for some real breakfast. Then we will take the shops of London by storm!"

* * *

Garrett had orchestrated everything for their comfort. Each of the ladies, including Dillie, was armed with a generous purse of pin money for any trinket that might catch her eye. Furthermore, Garrett directed the coachman to several of the town's best modistes, who had already been alerted to send the bills to him. The ladies were treated royally as they progressed through the day of reckless spending. Putty, resplendent in his livery, perched proudly on the back of the carriage.

The day continued fine, and Missy found it impossible not to be caught up in the pleasurable pursuit of the perfect gown. Laughing, she protested when Felicity pushed a length of sapphire blue silk into her arms, but the others insisted it was the perfect color for a ball gown, and was not, as Missy suggested, too bold.

Angelica, much to the surprise of the two sisters, was not the spoiled beauty she had portrayed the previous day. She entered into their undertaking with wholehearted enthusiasm, always knowing just the right ribbon or lace to finish out a gown and make it stunning.

Dillie, they soon discovered, was full of sage advice and keen insights. For an elderly spinster, she seemed to know a great deal about what the gentlemen might find attractive, and what they might find disagreeable.

By the middle of the afternoon, all four ladies were weary and greeted with enthusiasm Dillie's suggestion of ices at Gunter's in Berkley Square. Putty helped each of them down, standing at attention beside the carriage while they went inside.

Felicity immediately ordered tea and cakes to be sent out to Putty and John Coachman.

"Oh, I needed that so much," said Miss Dill, holding her tea cup in both her bony hands and taking a sip.

"This is lovely," whispered Felicity, looking around in awe at the elegant customers. "I will be so glad when we have our new gowns, Missy."

"But you look every bit as pretty as the other ladies here," said her sister.

"It is kind of you to say so, but I can't help feeling a little shabby in this old gown. Why, next to Angelica, I look the veriest dowd."

"Of course you don't," said Angelica, preening all the same. "And just wait until we attend a ball together. We will be a striking pair, both being tall."

"Believe me, girls, you will all take the town by storm! Here is Missy, a veritable pocket Venus, and the two of you, so graceful and elegant. I declare I have never had such a Season since my own in . . . oh, whenever it was."

"Tell us, Dillie, did you *take*?" asked Missy.

"Well, I did and I didn't. You wouldn't know it now, but I was quite a beauty then. I had, shall we say, charms that the gentlemen seemed to set great store by."

The three girls exchanged grins at this revelation. Looking at Dillie's bony frame, it was difficult to imagine her having enticing curves.

"Go on," said Angelica.

"Well, there was a certain gentleman who everyone believed was going to ask my father for permission to wed me."

"And did he?" asked Felicity, her smooth brow puckering with a sympathetic frown.

"Yes, but he was killed in a duel two days later. I never knew what that was about, but it quite devastated me, as you might imagine. Our betrothal appeared in the papers on the same day as the duel, so I had to retire to the country, of course, and that was that."

"Did you never get to return to London for another Season?"

"Oh, I found other things to occupy my time," said the old woman, smiling secretly, but she would not be drawn into further disclosures.

"Good afternoon, ladies," said Ian Emery, smiling at the ladies each in turn. "May I join you? There don't seem to be any other tables."

"Of course, Mr. Emery," said Felicity, speaking up quickly and moving her chair so that he could move another one into their circle.

"You are all looking lovely this afternoon," he said, though his eyes remained fixed on Felicity, who blushed prettily.

"And so are you," said Miss Dill, earning a quizzical expression from all her listeners. "If a gentleman is going to give me a compliment, I believe I should return the favor. Besides, Mr. Emery is looking especially handsome. Is that a new waistcoat?" she asked.

"Yes, as a matter of fact, it is, Miss Dill. How very observant of you."

"A lady notices these things. Isn't that so, Felicity?" she added coyly.

Felicity didn't know where to look, but Angelica

came to the rescue with a mocking, "I'm sure Mr. Emery believes every woman notices him."

"Angelica!" gasped Dillie and Felicity simultaneously.

But Mr. Emery would not be drawn into any argument. Turning, he ordered a cup of tea, ignoring Angelica's barb and sending her into the sulks.

"Have you enjoyed seeing all the shops, Miss Felicity?" asked Ian.

"Yes, it has been a lovely day. I had no idea there were so many colors, so many different types of cloth," said Felicity, turning the full force of her smile on the gentleman.

Reluctantly, he tore his eyes away, saying, "And you ladies haven't been to St. Bartholomew's bazaar yet. My sister swears you can buy anything there. But you must beware of pickpockets."

"Oh, I don't think I would like to go there," said Felicity.

"But it is a sight you shouldn't miss while you are here in London, Miss Felicity. Allow me to offer my services as escort," he added, his eyes for her alone.

Dillie cleared her throat, and Ian added, "To all of you ladies, of course."

The awkwardness passed, but Missy watched the pair closely. She had never known her sister to blush so readily, nor to play the coquette. Certainly at home Felicity never had the opportunity to practice the art of flirtation; they seldom attended social events, and then the topic of conversation, when Missy was nearby, was sure to be about horses.

Ian Emery seemed just as taken with Felicity as she was with him. Missy smiled. She hadn't expected it to be so easy for Felicity to find a man who took her fancy. If things went well with Ian Emery, she might see her little sister wed by autumn and be back at home well before Christmas.

She would mention the possibility of a match between Felicity and Mr. Emery to Garrett. He would be delighted, she was sure. Their guardian certainly seemed quite taken with Felicity, indulging her like a favorite daughter. He would probably be pleased to have her wed his best friend.

"What do you think, Missy?" inquired Felicity.

"I'm sorry; I was woolgathering. What did you ask?" Missy replied.

"I wondered if you thought we could be ready as early as next week to attend Mr. Emery's card party."

"My sister's card party, to be precise, although her husband is still in the country, and she has asked me to play host. Just a small affair. I thought it would allow Miss Felicity to become acquainted with some other young people on a less formal occasion than, say, a ball."

"I think that is a splendid idea," said Missy. "But now I think we should be going home. Dillie is quite worn out, I see, and I'm sure we could all do with a little rest before dinner."

Ian followed them out the door and helped Dillie and Missy into the heavily laden carriage. Angelica followed, leaving Felicity on the sidewalk with Ian.

"Well, you ladies have had a busy morning. I don't think there's enough room for you, Miss Felicity," he said.

"We can have some of these packages put in the

boot, and we'll hold some of them on our laps," said Missy, beginning to rearrange the entire pile.

"There is no need for that, Miss Lambert. I would be only too happy to bring your sister in my curricle. It is just across the street. If Miss Felicity doesn't mind, that is."

"Oh, no, not at all. You are most kind," said Felicity.

Missy looked doubtful, but it was an open carriage, just as Garrett had advised.

"I suppose it would be proper," she said. "What do you say, Dillie?"

"I see you have your tiger with you, Mr. Emery. Yes, yes, most proper," said the older woman, winking at the gentleman.

"Very well, but follow directly behind us. Thank you, Mr. Emery," said Missy, ignoring Putty, who was tugging on her sleeve.

"Happy to be of service," said Ian, offering his arm to Felicity.

"Do you want me t' go with Miss Felicity?" asked Putty.

"No, that won't be necessary, Putty. Mr. Emery's tiger will ride on the back. Miss Felicity will be fine," said Missy. Grumbling, the giant climbed onto the back of the carriage.

It didn't take long for Missy to realize the impossibility of keeping the two carriages together.

"Can you see Mr. Emery's curricle?" she called to the coachman.

"No, miss, it's too crowded. I saw 'im turn off back there a ways. He'll show up sooner or later. Mr. Emery's an accomplished whip. Miss Felicity's in good hands with him," said the driver, turning his attention back to the congested road.

Missy settled back against the soft cushions, putting any worries from her mind as she listened to Angelica and Dillie discuss the day's purchases. She didn't know how they could already be planning the next orgy of shopping. She was utterly exhausted!

When they arrived back at the elegant town house, Missy climbed the stairs to her chamber and sank into the nearest chair, pulling off her bonnet and gloves and tossing them on the bed. She shook the pins from her hair, which tumbled about her shoulders like a dark waterfall.

James, the awkward young footman, entered with her packages, and the maid, Dulcie, was right behind him with a tray of cool lemonade and biscuits. Missy smiled, thanking them both before dismissing them. Then she removed her shoes and stockings, wriggling her toes in the thick carpet and stretching in a most unladylike fashion.

Missy rose and ambled over to the table where the boxes had been neatly stacked. The first one held a straw bonnet she had allowed the others to press on her, though it was not in her usual style, being trimmed with pink rosebuds and white lace ribbons. It was very feminine, very frivolous, unlike the usual tailored styles she favored. Still, it would be very stylish and would turn the rose silk carriage dress she had ordered into a work of art.

Next was a mannish shako she had snapped up immediately to go with her favorite habit. The black hat was embellished with black and gold braid, an exact match for the habit.

As Missy continued to sort through her purchases, she marveled at the amount of clothes she had ordered and all the necessary accessories. Normally, she was content with a new gown every year or two, as long as she had good riding boots and a serviceable riding cape. Something was happening to her, and she wasn't entirely certain she liked it.

What would she do when this Season was over? She had never had any intention of marrying; her horses were all she had ever wanted. Of course, her father's will had spoiled her wish; the will had taken Lambert Racing Stables from her, after she had worked so hard to make it a success. All she now possessed, all that truly belonged to her, was King's Shilling. The will also stipulated that she could reside in the Dower house as long as she lived. But the stables, the land she loved, were now in the hands of her guardian.

Guardian! The word filled her with ire, making her forget how kind he seemed to be. He was still her guardian. The word made her forget all about her vow to be agreeable for Felicity's sake. She would cheerfully have strangled Garrett Wyndridge at that moment had the opportunity presented itself.

There was a knock on the door leading to Felicity's room, and Missy called forcefully, "Come in," before she turned back to the boxes, opening one that contained gloves for Felicity as well as for herself.

"Here, Felicity. I think these are yours," she said, turning to face her sister. Only it wasn't Felicity standing in her room, it was Sir Garrett Wyndridge, her *guardian*.

"What do you want?" she snapped before remembering her vow to be pleasant to the man.

His brows shot up in surprise, but he replied mildly, "I was looking for your sister, actually. I understand Ian drove her home."

"Yes; we were rather crowded," said Missy, sensing his displeasure but unsure of the reason behind it. "I assure you he made the offer to us; we didn't impose upon him. And after all, he is your friend," she added defensively.

"Indeed, yes. However, he is not . . . that is, he is not totally suitable as an escort for a young innocent such as Felicity," said Garrett, shifting uncomfortably from one foot to the other.

"Not suitable? In what way?"

"Oh, he is a decent enough fellow—a capital chap, as a matter of fact; it is just that . . . his reputation with the ladies—"

"He is a fortune hunter!" gasped Missy.

"No, no, nothing like that! He's flush in the pocket; Ian has no need to marry for money," said Garrett, grimacing beneath his ward's relentless glare. "It's just that he is a bit of a rake."

With a derisive snort, Missy snarled, "You invite a hardened rake and libertine into your home, introduce him to your eighteen-year-old ward, and don't bother to warn anyone? And I thought *we* were the country bumpkins!"

"Missy, it is not as bad as all that. I have no reason to think that anything untoward has happened. They are probably taking a drive through the park. It is the fashionable hour."

"So now you are telling me that my little sister's first appearance in Society will be in the curricle of a practiced flirt who is quite capable of winning her heart and then breaking it in two," said Missy, stalking over to wag her finger under his nose.

"Oh, surely Felicity has more sense than to take anything Ian says seriously," said Garrett.

Missy dropped her hand and turned away, her frown deepening. She sighed and shook her head before facing him again. "You would not be saying that had you seen how she looked at him when we met him at Gunter's Confectionery. I am afraid she has already formed a tendre for the man."

"Pish and tush!" declared Felicity, flouncing into the room.

"My dear! When did you arrive home?"

"At least ten minutes ago. I was speaking to Turtle about his arthritis. I told him about putting the copper beneath his mattress. I thought it might help him like it did Mrs. Cooper back home. Now, what are you two doing alone in Missy's bedchamber?"

Garrett began backing toward the door. "Nothing, Felicity, nothing at all. I only just stepped in for a moment. To speak to her . . . I . . . I'll see you both at dinner."

When he had gone, Felicity turned her inquiring gaze on her sister. Missy met her eyes unwaveringly.

"We were both concerned when you and Mr. Emery became separated from us. Garrett thought perhaps you had turned into the park for a drive."

"No; we came straight home, but Ian—Mr. Emery, that is—took a different route. I saw some of the most incredible houses, Missy, even grander than this one," said Felicity, her gay prattle fooling no one.

"It won't do, you know," said Missy.

"What?"

"Mr. Emery is a fine gentleman, but he does have a reputation as a rake, a confirmed bachelor who likes to lead the ladies on with no intention of marriage."

Felicity tossed her blond curls and looked down at her petite older sister with pursed lips.

"I care nothing for Mr. Emery's reputation with the ladies, Missy. He is our guardian's friend; that is all. I have no designs on him, just as I am certain he has none on me. He was the perfect gentleman. I care nothing for his past; as long as he treats me with respect and kindness, I will stand his friend also." With stately tread, she left the room, softly closing the connecting door between the two bedchambers.

Missy shook her head sadly. It was obvious, at least to her, that her little sister was close to being head over heels in love with Mr. Ian Emery. It was equally obvious that Felicity had no intention of admitting this to herself or anyone else.

Ah, well, such was the way of love. At least, that was what all the books and plays Missy had read said about love. She had never experienced it herself.

She had once fancied herself in love with Price, the steward's son. They had known each other all their lives, but he had suddenly seemed interesting and exciting when he returned from Eton at the age of sixteen. Then she had grown used to him again, their wrangling had recommenced, and she had felt no more pangs of calf-love.

What Felicity was feeling was probably much the same. Given a week or two, she would put such nonsense from her mind.

She was a sensible girl and would understand that,

in addition to being a rake, the man was ten years her senior if he was a day. Why, Ian Emery wasn't even handsome! He was tall and lanky, with a head of red hair and a sprinkling of freckles across his sharp nose. Charm could only go so far, and Felicity was much too beautiful to settle for one such as Ian Emery.

Missy walked across the room and sat down in front of the mirror to brush her hair. Really studying her image, she noticed the tumbling curls, looked down at her bare feet, and felt the color rush to her cheeks. Garrett! What must he think of her, conversing with him half dressed?

In his chamber in the east wing, Garrett snapped at his valet and ordered a bath before dinner. A cool bath. Anderson grumbled something vile about slave-driving employers, but he stalked out of the room to do as he was bid.

Sinking into the tepid water, Garrett expelled a frustrated groan. How the devil was he going to survive the entire Season with Missy Lambert under his roof, cutting up his peace every time he set eyes on her? They had only conversed a half-dozen times, and hadn't made it through one conversation without him losing his composure. There was just something about the girl that made him want to shake her!

This gratifying image transformed without warning into his arms encircling her completely and pulling her against his chest, his hands plunging into those sensuous, thick curls.

"Blast!" She was his ward, for heaven's sake!

But the thought of her with those silken curls free, bounding about her shoulders, made him moan with frustration all over again. And the feet . . . those slender, bare feet . . .

Garrett chuckled despite himself. She had no idea of the effect she had on him. She had been completely oblivious of the irresistible image she presented.

Anderson entered and poured another pail of water into the tub, dousing Garrett and his reveries.

It really doesn't matter how Missy looked, he reminded himself. *She is your ward, and you are her guardian.*

But that hair. . . .

"Oh, the devil take her! The devil take them all!" growled Garrett, causing his retreating valet to drop the empty pail with a loud clang.

"I beg your pardon, sir?" said the servant.

"Lay out my evening clothes, Anderson. I shall be going to the club this evening; inform Turtle that I shan't be dining at home after all."

"Very good, sir."

Ian Emery dined at Watier's almost every night since his sister's arrival in London had forced him to take bachelor lodgings. Garrett had no trouble finding his friend, but once he had joined him at table and ordered his own dinner, he fell into a morose silence. Ian was not his usual garrulous self either.

Finally, peeling a pear for his dessert, Ian advised, "Say what you want, Garrett. Just get it over with."

Green eyes met blue in silent understanding.

"She's too young for me," supplied Ian.

"And too innocent," added Garrett, carefully avoiding the use of Felicity's name in this gentlemen's haunt.

"And certainly too good for me. She wants someone as fresh and good as she is, not an old dog such as me."

"Exactly," agreed Garrett, rising. "So we understand each other on that point?"

"Just tell me one thing, Garrett. If I were to ignore your warning, if I were to pursue the lady . . ."

"I'd have to call you out," Garrett said.

They exchanged smiles to show they both appreciated the absurdity of his threat. Garrett could cup a wafer at fifty yards, and his swordplay was legendary. To meet him on the field of honor was nothing short of suicide.

Garrett turned to go, but Ian stopped him with his quiet question, "If it came to that, who would the lady mourn? You or me?"

Garrett looked over his shoulder and replied, "Knowing her kind heart, both of us, old friend. Both of us." Then he walked away.

Ian called for a second bottle and proceeded to get very drunk, something he hadn't done since his salad days.

Four

Missy kept a close watch over her sister for several days, but Felicity didn't appear to be pining for the unattainable Mr. Emery. They seldom saw him, and when they met, their exchanges were innocuous. Relieved that her sister had escaped heart whole from that escapade, Missy began a quiet exploration for a suitable husband for her beautiful, giving sister.

Garrett encouraged his wards to continue their shopping spree. The activity brought a grateful smile from Felicity, kept the tantrum-prone Angelica happy, and had the added advantage of keeping the disturbing Missy Lambert out of his way.

It was not that he could think of nothing else but Missy; rather, it was easier to keep such unsuitable thoughts at bay if she was not forever popping up under his nose. Mornings were no problem; he formed the habit of avoiding the stables until Missy and Putty had returned from their ride. He had purchased two ladies' hacks, but Missy refused to switch from Tucker. Grudgingly, Garrett had to admit she was an intrepid horsewoman; she never again allowed the mare to have her own way.

They managed to avoid solitary confrontations in

the morning since Missy never came downstairs to break her fast. Garrett wondered if this was by design or if it had always been her habit to breakfast in her room. Regardless, he appreciated being able to eat in peace with only his morning paper for company. In the evening, dinner was not as difficult with everyone present.

One week after their arrival, most of their new wardrobes had been completed, and Dillie pronounced Missy and Felicity ready for Society. They would have their first chance at a card party given by Ian's sister, Lady Margaret Warnham, who had come by for tea one day to extend the invitation personally. She was a straightforward matron with red hair, darker than her brother's, but she was short and round in figure. Missy and Felicity liked her immediately, though Angelica and Lady Margaret were barely on speaking terms.

The big evening finally arrived, and Missy donned one of her new gowns, an ivory silk with tiny puffed sleeves and a low decolletage. She would have ordered the modiste to fill this void with lace, but everyone, including Dillie, had quashed the idea. So Missy now regarded her reflection with dismay.

"With my hair in a coil on top of my head, there appears to be entirely too much of me showing," she protested.

"Nonsense. You look very elegant," said Felicity, giving her sister's coiffure a final pat. "It lends you height, and Mama's pearls are the perfect accessory."

Turning her head this way and that, Missy quipped, "I only hope the pins do not decide to come loose; I might break my neck when the coil unwinds."

Felicity frowned and replied gravely, "I don't think it will happen, but you mustn't turn your head too quickly. Thank heavens there will be no dancing this evening. That might really jog something loose."

"I shall pretend to be a statue, shall I?" said Missy, drawing on the long matching gloves. "Did Cousin Garrett decide to accompany us?" she asked casually.

"Yes; he promised at lunch that he would do so. I am quite looking forward to tonight, Missy, but I hope I don't do anything stupid at the card table."

Angelica sailed into the room, a vision in pale pink sprigged muslin. Catching the end of Felicity's statement, she said, "Just remember to giggle, Felicity. That's all it takes."

"And I suppose you know all about it," snapped Felicity. Immediately she apologized, saying, "Please forgive me, Angelica. I am suffering from a case of nerves. I am so afraid I will make a mistake. I know it is only Silver Loo, but I am not very good at games that involve wagering."

"But you and Papa played piquet all the time," said Missy.

"Yes, but that was different. I wasn't losing real money."

"Never fear, Felicity," said Missy. "This is one thing I know about from going to the races every year. When a lady makes a poor wager, she just giggles and says she should have asked him for advice, whoever the 'him' is: father, brother, husband, suitor. They forgive her immediately and give her even more money, no matter how many times it happens."

"Really?" asked Felicity. "I find it hard to believe they could be so foolish!"

"Men? They think they are much more quick-witted than we are, Felicity," said the worldly Angelica. With a wicked grin, she added, "When in doubt, just simper, sigh, or giggle. It works every time."

"How lowering," Felicity whispered to Missy as they followed Angelica down the hall.

Garrett was waiting at the foot of the stairs, dressed in evening clothes with only a solitary emerald relieving the severity of his black coat and snowy cravat.

He is the most handsome man I have ever seen, thought Missy as she felt an odd fluttering in her stomach. *Nerves, only nerves,* she thought, *just like Felicity.*

Dillie, who stood beside Garrett, said loudly, "You see how well we have spent your money, my boy."

"Indeed, it was well worth it," he replied, smiling as he greeted each of his wards in turn. When he spoke to Missy, he lifted her hand to his lips for a chaste salute. His voice low, he added, "A veritable bevy of beauties, my ladies."

"You look very beautiful, too," said Felicity, grinning up at him.

"Felicity!" hissed Angelica. "A lady doesn't say such things to a gentleman."

"Nonsense. Dillie said it was perfectly proper to compliment a gentleman on his appearance."

"Proper and flattering," said Garrett. "And I thank you, Felicity. I thought I should try to look my best since I would be escorting such lovely ladies."

Angelica winked at Felicity and giggled. Garrett shot her a quizzical glance and offered his arm to Dillie, who thrust out her bony chest and led the way to the carriage.

"I thought perhaps I should ride; I don't wish to

crush your gowns," said Garrett, helping Dillie into the equipage.

"This is such a large carriage, Garrett, and Felicity and Angelica are so slender, we should fit nicely. I will sit with them in the forward-facing seat, if you don't mind sitting with Missy in the rear-facing seat?" asked Dillie, very much in charge of the situation.

"If you think it best," acquiesced Garrett. "And if Missy doesn't mind sitting with me."

"Not at all," she said quietly.

While the two younger girls chattered excitedly, Missy and Garrett sat silently as they made their way from Portman to Grosvenor where Lady Margaret and her husband lived.

The house was ablaze with lamps and candles, the light spilling onto the roadway. Garrett hopped to the ground first, then turned to assist Dillie and his wards. Missy exited last, stifling a gasp when his hands went about her waist as he swung her to the ground.

"You were so quiet on the way over, Missy. Are you feeling all right?" asked Garrett, frowning in concern.

Missy nodded and waited for him to release her. Finally, he dropped his hands and offered her his arm. When she placed her hand on his sleeve, he covered her hand with his, the simple, protective gesture causing the butterflies in her stomach to take flight once again, robbing her of any ability to speak in a rational manner.

There was no receiving line for the informal gathering, but Lady Margaret soon discovered their presence and presented them to numerous people.

"Now, I don't know how well you play, but I

thought you ladies might prefer to be paired with more experienced players for the first few hands; that way they can demonstrate how to place wagers and so on."

"What a good idea," said Felicity happily.

"Garrett, I know you won't mind joining Lord Amhearst and Lady Shelton. They prefer whist to loo, you know. And Miss Lambert, if you wouldn't mind being his partner?"

"Of course. Thank you, Maggie," said Garrett, using her childhood name just as her brother did.

"Miss Wyndridge, you are acquainted with Mr. Preston, I believe. He has been asking for you this past hour. And, Miss Dill, I believe you know Admiral Tupperman?"

"Dear Tupper! Where have you been hiding for the past ten years?" asked Dillie, latching onto the admiral and chattering like a schoolgirl. "And you're an admiral now. How famous!"

"That leaves only you, Miss Felicity. My brother was here a few minutes . . . ah, there you are, Ian. Would you be a dear and show Miss Felicity how to go on?"

"I would be delighted," said Ian, leading Felicity away to one of the farthest tables.

Missy and Garrett exchanged speaking glances, but there was nothing they could do. Play resumed, and Missy accompanied Garrett to their assigned table.

"Good evening, Wyndridge," said the elderly gentleman, rising and giving Missy a courtly bow.

"Good evening, Amhearst, Lady Shelton. May I present my, uh, cousin, Miss Lambert? Missy, this is Lady Shelton and Lord Amhearst."

"How do you do?" murmured Missy, taking a seat opposite Garrett's place.

"You wouldn't be the late Baron Lambert's daughter now, would you?" asked Lord Amhearst.

"Yes, my lord."

"Fine man. Knew his way around a stable," said the elderly gentleman.

Missy smiled and thanked him.

"Well, what say you to a rubber of whist?" said Lord Amhearst. "I warn you, though, Sylvia and I take no prisoners when we play whist."

"I don't mind," said Garrett. "Do you know the game, Missy?"

"Not very well, but I will try, if you promise not to lose your patience with me," she said.

"Lose my patience? Don't be silly," replied Garrett. "Deal the cards, Amhearst."

Missy soon realized that play, and very little conversation, was the order of the evening as the game became more and more intense. Though his words and actions gave no indication, Missy could sense Garrett's absorption in the game growing with each play.

Missy played her last card and watched Lady Shelton gather in the trick. A tiny muscle beside Garrett's mouth twitched, but he laughed, saying, "Never mind about this hand, Missy. We'll do better the next hand. Care to up the stakes a little, Amhearst?"

"Certainly, if you can bear the loss, Wyndridge."

"I don't intend to lose," said Garrett, arranging his hand as Lord Amhearst turned over the queen of hearts for trumps.

Garrett winked at Missy, or she thought he did. Perhaps it was just another nervous tic. Missy laid down the jack of spades. Garrett frowned, then gave her another wink and nodded.

The first trick went to Lady Shelton. Play continued, with few hearts being led; Garrett's frown grew as the stack of tricks beside Lady Shelton's elbow did. Finally, Garrett had the lead, and he played the nine of hearts. Missy played the ten, causing him to frown even more fiercely as she took the trick.

Missy studied her cards nervously. "Piquet is really my game," she said with a choking sound.

"Just lead anything," said her partner confidently. "All we need is two more tricks."

Two out of three. He knew he had the cards to win two of them. They couldn't lose. All she had to do was lead a club or a spade, or even the. . . .

"Ace of hearts!" barked Garrett. "What the devil are you doing with the ace of hearts?"

"Garrett, old man, mustn't shout at the ladies," said Amhearst, laying a hand on Garrett's sleeve.

The muscles in his jaw worked overtime as he gave up his king of hearts, but he said nothing. Amhearst pulled out his jack on the next trick, changed the lead to clubs, and took the last trick, too.

"I'm sorry, Garrett," said Missy, wide-eyed.

She remembered Angelica's advice to giggle, but somehow it didn't seem to be the right time. She wanted to. Oh, she wanted to laugh out loud. Finally, she had discovered a chink in her guardian's gleaming armor. He was a spoilsport. Oh, he didn't have a tantrum, but he was definitely having trouble controlling his temper. He wanted to win so very badly.

Missy bit her lip to keep from grinning as the most

wicked thought crossed her mind. What would Garrett do if they lost the next hand, too?

"Refreshments, everyone," announced Lady Margaret, flitting from table to table.

Garrett rose and stalked away. Lord Amhearst crooked both his elbows and led Missy and Lady Shelton to the dining room.

Garrett was downing his second glass of champagne by the time Missy reached the buffet tables. He watched her cross the room, her ivory silk gown floating around her ankles. She wore tiny silk rosebuds in her dark hair and held her head as regally as a queen. She was so perfect and so petite, he thought, unable to tear his eyes from her.

She spotted him and smiled. Turning to Lord Amhearst, she said something and crossed the room to Garrett.

"I am sorry, Garrett," she said, her grin anything but remorseful.

"I bet you are," he replied, relaxing as he answered her smile. How could he help but forgive her? She was too lovely for him to remain angry. Still smiling, he asked, "Why didn't you tell me you were so dreadful at cards?"

"I really didn't realize I was. I almost never played cards. Felicity and Papa often played piquet, but I just wasn't interested. I suppose I should have paid attention," she added, giggling.

"We'll see that you have lessons. There are ways to signal your partner what cards you're holding."

"But isn't that cheating?" asked Missy.

"Not at all. The way you lead out tells your partner what you have. For instance, when you are holding the ace of trumps and four or five lesser trumps, you do not, I repeat, do not, lead with some other suit."

"Really? Why ever not? I thought it would be wise to save my trumps," said Missy, her brow puckering adorably as she pondered this puzzle.

Garrett roared with laughter and took her arm, leading her back to the buffet tables that were sagging under the weight of all sorts of delicacies.

"Never mind," he said, selecting a grape and offering it to her. Missy opened her mouth obediently and he placed it on her tongue. "You may play any way you wish."

"But, Garrett, I would like to improve, you know."

"Then we'll have lessons with your sister and Dillie, with buttons for wagers," he said, picking up a plate and beginning to fill it.

By the end of the evening, Garrett and Missy had won several hands, though they lost all the rubbers. Missy knew they had been beaten soundly when Lord Amhearst and Lady Shelton offered to play against them again, any time, anywhere. But Garrett didn't lose his temper again. If Missy played the wrong card, he patiently explained after the hand why she should have made a different play.

By the time they had climbed back into their carriage, Missy's opinion of her guardian had risen to new heights. She still refused to admit that she needed a guardian, but she supposed Garrett wasn't such a bad one.

And though he had acted the spoilsport at first, he had recovered nicely, even complimenting her on her progress as the evening had worn on. All in all, she had enjoyed their first outing into Society.

She started to ask Felicity if she had enjoyed herself, but the look on her shining face, readable each
time they passed a streetlamp, told its own story. Missy
frowned.

When they arrived at the town house, Garrett said,
"Missy, a word with you, if you please."

She followed him to the rear of the house and into
his study. Evidently, Garrett usually came into his
study for a drink after an evening out, for a small fire
was burning merrily in the grate and the decanters
and glasses were waiting.

"Would you like a sherry?" he asked, pouring his
own glass of brandy.

"No, thank you," said Missy, sitting down on the
worn leather sofa.

Garrett joined her there. He held the snifter in
both hands and swirled it gently. Missy noticed for
the first time the tiny lines at the corners of his eyes;
he had spent many hours in the sun. His dark lashes
would have been the envy of any girl; they were long
and curled. Then he turned those eyes on her, and
she felt her heart skip a beat.

How foolish, she thought. She had read the phrase
in books, but she had never experienced it before. *It
hadn't really skipped a beat,* asserted her logical side.

Grinning, Garrett asked, "What is it? You have the
most open face, Missy. You must never play cards for
large sums of money. Your opponents would always
know what you were holding in your hand."

"Is that what you wanted to talk to me about?"
Missy retorted.

"No, not at all. I wanted to ask if you think I should

speak to Ian again. Or to Felicity. She . . . she looked so vulnerable when we left," he said.

Missy warmed to him again; how kind of him to notice her sister's state.

"I don't want her to be hurt," Garrett added.

"Neither do I, but I'm afraid it's not in our hands, Garrett. Mr. Emery has done nothing to encourage her, unless one counts being charming. No, Felicity will have to work this out for herself."

Missy stood up. Getting to his feet, Garrett said, "Very well, if you say so, Missy. But let me know if there is anything I can do to help, won't you?"

"Certainly, Garrett. Good night."

"Good night," he replied, resuming his seat when she had walked to the door.

Missy turned and studied him for another moment, setting the image firmly in her mind, the way the firelight turned his face to gold, the dark curl that fell across his brow.

Tears sprang to her eyes; she didn't know why. She didn't want to know why. Hurrying to her room, all Missy knew was she wanted to go home. More than anything, she needed to go home.

Climbing into bed some time later, she swiped angrily at her foolish tears. Her head ached slightly; she tried to tell herself she must be ill. But the truth, though she wouldn't allow herself to believe it, throbbed in her brain: How could she bear to go home alone? How could she bear it?

Evenings had become a whirl of activities as the ladies trekked from one entertainment to the next, sometimes attending four or five gatherings in one night.

Felicity, who appeared completely recovered from her infatuation with Mr. Emery, was well on the way to being the belle of the Season. Though Miss Hadley was perhaps prettier and Miss Simmons the more vivacious, Felicity outshone both of them in manner and temperament. For her there was none of the bored indifference, the feigned sophistication; where Felicity went, the delight she took in the ball or rout was infectious. Soon, everyone who entered her sphere shared her glow of pleasure and enchantment.

And Missy watched from the sidelines, enjoying a modest success for herself, enough to be gratifying, but no one came forward to sweep her off her feet and make her forget her plans.

"She is the Season's favorite, Miss Lambert," said Ian Emery, appearing at Missy's elbow as she watched the dancers at yet another ball.

"I had no doubt that she would be," said Missy, smiling.

"You are to be congratulated," he said, his voice laced with a touch of melancholy. At her quizzical glance, he added, "It is wonderful that your sister, being the beauty she is, has no consciousness of her appearance. She is completely unaffected."

"I take no credit for Felicity's good sense and manners, Mr. Emery. Rather, they are as natural to her as her beauty is. But I do take joy in knowing that she is appreciated, so I thank you," said Missy.

"Good evening, Garrett," said Ian, shaking hands

with his friend, who had torn himself away from the card room long enough to watch the dancing.

"Hello, Ian," said Garrett, watching the dancers for a moment before turning back to Missy and saying, "Why are you not dancing, Missy?"

"I have been, which you would know if you ever bothered to leave the card room, sir. I choose not to waltz. It seems much too familiar a dance."

"I think you mean you do not know the steps," taunted Garrett, his smile issuing a challenge.

"I mean that I have no desire to be bundled about by some so-called gentleman I have only just met," came the tart reply.

Ian chuckled.

"So if someone whom you knew well were to ask you to waltz, you would agree to it," said Garrett.

"But I don't know anyone in London that well," said Missy.

"You know me," said Garrett triumphantly before he could ask himself what the deuce he thought he was doing requesting a dance—a waltz—of his ward, the one who never failed to make him uncomfortable!

"And me," said Ian, bowing before Missy. "Miss Lambert, may I be the first to have the honor of a waltz?"

Missy opened her mouth to deny his request, but she glanced at Garrett, whose mocking grin had transformed into a deep scowl, and she said, "I would love to, Mr. Emery. How kind of you to ask. Shall we?"

With a grin for his friend, Ian took Missy's hand

and guided her smoothly into the swirling mass of dancers, one hand at her waist.

"That's it," said Ian encouragingly. "I see Garrett was quite wrong when he accused you of not knowing the steps. You waltz very well."

"Thank you, Mr. Emery. And so do you."

"Ah, but such is the duty of a rake and a libertine," he teased. "To ply my trade, I must be a master of all the social niceties."

"I don't think you are such a rake, Mr. Emery. You have always acted the gentleman with us."

"*Acted* being the key word, Miss Lambert. A man may act any way he chooses; that does not alter what he is."

"A wolf in sheep's clothing? I don't know if I believe you. And even if I do, can a man not change?" she asked.

"Perhaps, but it is unlikely. And for me, I find it is better to know one's shortcomings," said Ian, halting as the final strains of the music faded away. He bowed low and said, "A short waltz. Good evening, Miss Lambert," before walking away.

"Is he gone then?" asked Felicity.

Missy looked up at her willowy sister in time to see the flash of pain that flitted across her eyes before her expression became guarded once again.

"Vouchers!" cried Angelica, swooping down on them and pulling Felicity and Missy to one side. "Lady Drummond-Burrell has promised to call on us tomorrow," she said, barely containing a squeal of excitement.

The two sisters gave her a perfunctory smile, causing Angelica to reiterate, "Vouchers to Almack's! Only think! Our Season is made!"

Angelica drifted away as if on a cloud; Missy and Felicity giggled.

"I know we are supposed to care about such nonsense, but it all seems rather silly to me," said Felicity.

"A great deal seems rather silly to me," agreed Missy. "I know we have been here for only two weeks, but I cannot imagine spending every spring in London for the Season."

"Oh, I don't know, Missy. It is very agreeable to dance, listen to music, and go to the theater. I think I might become quite used to it. As long as I have a home in the country for the other times of the year. Yes, I think I could become very used to this sort of life," said Felicity, smiling at her next partner.

Missy watched her go, shaking her head. It was a good thing, she told herself, that Felicity felt the way she did. She would marry and be able to lead the type of life she claimed to love. And Missy. . . .

She felt a wave of frustration. What was she doing here in London, hundreds of miles from her home, hundreds of miles from her horse? She wondered how the groom was doing with King's Shilling. The young stallion was still so skittish; he was not at all ready for racing, but when Newmarket came, he had to be ready. He was her only hope. If King's Shilling was still too jumpy to be around crowds, she wouldn't be able to enter him in the race, and she wouldn't win the money necessary to begin her own stables. If he won, the demand for him as a stud would be enough to keep them going.

Dillie tapped her on the arm and said anxiously,

"Missy, where is Angelica? I saw her heading for the doors to the balcony a few minutes ago on the arms of two gentlemen, but she is not out there now."

"I haven't seen her," said Missy.

"You don't suppose she went into the gardens with them, do you? Oh, she will ruin her reputation for sure," said the old woman, wringing her hands. "And Cousin Garrett will turn me out of the house, and you and—"

"Now, now. I will go and find her. Wait here and calm down, Dillie. I'm sure nothing of the sort has happened."

"Thank you, dear, thank you," said the older woman.

Missy made her way indirectly toward the balcony doors, hoping no one noticed she was on a mission. She slipped outside and took a deep breath. The evening was a bit chilly so she pulled the silk shawl about her narrow shoulders. Dillie was right about one thing. Angelica and her escorts had not lingered on the balcony.

She allowed her eyes time to grow accustomed to the dim lights of the garden. Really, Lady Higgins, their hostess, had provided ample lighting for the pathways. Surely there could be nothing wrong with a stroll. From her elevated vantage point, she could easily detect the movements of several guests strolling here and there by the light of numerous Chinese lanterns swaying from the trees and shrubbery.

Shaking her head at the absurdity of Society's rules, Missy tripped lightly down the stone steps and into the garden. As she progressed farther and farther along the pathway, she had to admit the lighting was growing more and more faint, the lanterns fewer and fewer. Her pace quickened as she heard Angelica's tinselly laugh.

"Lud, Mr. Worth, you are being naughty," she said. Missy groaned.

"Then you'll grant my wish for the second waltz, dear Angelica?" came a deep voice.

"No!" said Missy, appearing on the scene to find Angelica with not one man, but two. She tempered her tone, adding, "That is, you know Miss Wyndridge can do no such thing, sir. Another dance, perhaps, but not another waltz. Isn't that right, Angelica?"

With a pout for Missy and a wink for Mr. Worth, Angelica said, "I suppose my cousin is right, sir."

"Then what about me, Miss Wyndridge? Say you'll grant me the next waltz," said an earnest young man who had a tendency to spots. Missy judged him to be about twenty-three or -four; he wore absurdly high shirt points that made turning his head almost impossible.

Angelica rapped his arm with her fan and trilled, "I suppose I could do that, Lord Thorpe, since you ask so prettily."

Even in the poor light, Missy could see the young man's blush of pleasure. Angelica took his arm, and they strolled back toward the house.

Mr. Worth extended his arm to Missy, saying, "We have not been formally introduced, Miss Lambert, but I feel I know you already."

"Oh, and why is that, Mr. Worth?" asked Missy, accepting his escort.

"Because I know your horses," said Worth, smiling down at her. "I even visited Lambert Farm once, but

I don't recall seeing you there. I would have remembered."

He was a handsome man. Not like Garrett, of course; no one could compare to him, but Mr. Worth's sandy hair and dark eyes were a pleasing combination. What's more, he seems a man of sense, thought Missy.

"You enjoy racing?" she asked.

"I enjoy watching the horses. I cannot claim to being a expert on them, but I do enjoy watching them run."

"And placing a wager or two?" teased Missy.

"Only small ones, I assure you, Miss Lambert. I am afraid my pockets are not as deep as your guardian's are. No, the pleasure for me is watching those great beasts throwing their hearts into the race, their legs churning, their necks outstretched. . . ." Chuckling, he dropped his arm and stopped on the path. "You must think me an absolute looby to go on like this, but it is a passion with me, you see. A race is like a beautiful woman; it fair takes my breath away."

Missy slowly expelled the breath she had been holding as she listened to the man's words. She shook her head and said huskily, "I assure you, Mr. Worth, I think nothing of the sort. In truth, I have never heard it articulated so eloquently. Your feelings so closely mirror my own that—"

"What the deuce is going on?" growled Garrett, taking Missy's hand and pulling her to his side while he glared at Mr. Worth.

Fitzsimmons Worth smiled at Garrett, but the expression didn't reach his eyes. Not that Missy noticed. She whirled on Garrett, her hand balled into a fist, her eyes blazing. Even in the dim light, Garrett could read her fury.

He put up one hand to forestall her outburst, saying hurriedly, "Dillie is wondering where you are."

Missy dropped her hand and turned, saying, "If you will forgive me, Mr. Worth, I must return to the festivities. We must continue our discussion another time."

"Worth," said Garrett, his eyes narrowed in dislike. He turned to follow Missy, taking her hand and placing it on his arm. He had to hold it there forcibly, for she would have snatched it away.

In a low whisper, he asked, "What did you think you were doing? Surely you are old enough to know a lady does not accept clandestine assignations. And certainly not with the likes of Fitzsimmons Worth. He's an out-and-out bounder!"

"He seems a very sensible gentleman to me. And what is more, Garrett Wyndridge, you have no right to censure my behavior!" snapped Missy.

"But I do. As your guardian . . ."

Missy jerked away from him. They had reached the balcony now where other couples lingered here and there.

"According to the law, you may be the guardian of my person, Sir Garrett, but you are not the guardian of my heart. I will decide with whom I shall converse. Not you!" she ground out before storming away.

"Damn," breathed Garrett, watching her until she disappeared from sight. He made his way to the card room, where he was sure to find something more substantial than the watery champagne Lady Higgins always served.

As for Missy, she could not stop the flow of tears. She didn't know why. Or rather, she didn't wish to delve into the reasons for her tears. The only thoughts she would allow, and these were not rational, was that Sir Garrett Wyndridge was an unreasonable cad, and that he could go to the devil, for all she cared. Some of the phrases she had picked up through years of working in the stables would have come in handy, but a young lady, dressed in the height of fashion, just didn't voice such sentiments. So she remained hidden in the ladies' withdrawing room, away from prying eyes, and from her loathsome guardian.

Felicity would come looking for her sooner or later, and then they could leave. The minutes ticked away slowly as the musicians played yet another tune. Finally, the door opened and she heard her sister's voice.

"In here, Felicity. I am not feeling well."

"Oh, Missy, I am sorry. You should have sent someone for me. Come, dearest. We will get you home."

"Thank you."

"I'll find Dillie and Angelica. I believe Cousin Garrett is in the card—"

"No! I don't wish to disturb the others. Just call the carriage. I can go home alone. There is no need to cut short your pleasure."

"I wouldn't hear of it! I will go with you. We'll send the carriage back for the others."

With this, Missy had to be satisfied. She gave her eyes another surreptitious swipe before following her sister out the door. Though she would have preferred a solitary ride, at least she wouldn't have to put up with Garrett's company. At least she wouldn't have to see his handsome face. As it was, she expected him to figure prominently in her dreams. *Nightmares were more like,* she thought, wadding up the sodden handkerchief in her fist.

Missy accepted her sister's ministrations when they were alone in her room. Tucked into bed like a child, Missy gave her sister a watery smile before she blew out the final candle.

Surprisingly, sleep came easily.

Garrett did figure prominently in her dreams, but they were not nightmares. Not until she awoke in the morning and remembered his sweet caresses and kisses. Groaning, Missy burrowed back under the covers.

No one had ever accused Missy Lambert of being a silly widgeon. Not until now. But that was the only appellation Missy could think of that fit so appropriately. Only a silly widgeon would be foolish enough to fall in love with the man she should abhor, the man who had her in his clutches.

Missy's treacherous mind flashed immediately back to her dreams. She groaned again.

Oh, but those clutches!

Five

The ladies in the elegant town house in Portman Square gathered around in awe to gaze at the four vouchers sent by Lady Drummond-Burrell. Miss Dill held them reverently, her eyes misting over with tears.

"We have arrived, girls," she announced grandly, her ramrod-straight back becoming, if possible, even more rigid.

"Will Cousin Garrett escort us?" asked Felicity.

"He must!" exclaimed Angelica.

"I think he might prefer to remain at home," said Missy. "I understand that for the gentlemen, knee breeches are de rigueur. Perhaps Cousin Garrett will object to such a costume."

"How can you say so, Missy? Your cousin has been all that he should. He will not desert you now, my dear."

If only he would, thought Missy sourly. It wasn't that she wouldn't enjoy his company, but her foolishness, as she now termed it, would take away from any pleasure she might feel in the evening. Almack's, even for her, was a name that commanded respect.

"Here he is now. We shall ask him," said Angelica.

"Ask me what?" queried Garrett, strolling toward

the sofa and chairs where the ladies were sitting with their needlework.

He must have been out riding, for he wore a bottle green riding coat and knitted tan riding breeches, his calves filling them out to perfection. His cravat was tied in an intricate waterfall, the elaborate concoction at odds with the clean lines of his coat and breeches. He was the epitome of elegance, thought Missy, edging her skirts to one side so he could join her on the sofa. She made a mental note to always sit in chairs from that point on.

"We were wondering if you will escort us to Almack's next Wednesday evening," said Felicity, her sweet smile charming him instantly. Even if he had planned to refuse, Missy could see that he would not now.

"I would be delighted, ladies. I am yours to command."

"You won't mind wearing knee breeches?" asked Missy hopefully.

"Not for you, my dears," he replied.

Was it her imagination, or had he made the word "dear" plural as an afterthought? wondered Missy. *What nonsense!* she added, chiding herself for more foolishness.

Missy had determined, by the time she and Putty had finished their silent ride that morning, that she was merely infatuated with Sir Garrett Wyndridge, just as Felicity was with Mr. Emery. She might be in danger of falling in love with the man, but she was definitely not in love with him yet. This small distinction allowed her to retain a small glimmer of hope that she had not completely lost the use of her faculties.

"Missy, Garrett was asking if we had our gowns picked out for Almack's yet," said Dillie, leaning over and tapping Missy's hand.

Missy almost gasped, her blue eyes flashing up to Garrett's face and then back down to her lap.

"Yes; yes, I have."

"Which one will you wear?" asked Felicity, completely unaware of the panic her questions were causing her sister.

"The, uh, blue one, I think," said Missy.

"The sapphire blue one?" asked Angelica. Missy nodded.

"Sapphire blue, is it?" said Garrett. "I look forward to seeing you in that, Missy. It should match your eyes beautifully."

Missy hoped the scarlet stain on her cheeks would be taken for embarrassment and not pleasure. She looked up sharply, a tentative smile on her lips.

But Garrett rose, saying, "If you ladies will excuse me. I have an engagement this afternoon, and I mustn't be late. Good day."

The cause of Missy's blush changed from pleasure to peevishness. The man was an unfeeling, arrogant beast! She loathed him, she told herself as he strode across the room and out the door.

Seconds later, the parlor door opened again, and Missy's heart skipped a beat. But it was only Turtle. Her heart returned to its normal progress.

Turtle was carrying a large bouquet of flowers which he placed on a narrow table next to the window.

"These just arrived for you, Miss Lambert," he said, bringing Missy the card before he left the room.

"Who are they from?" asked Felicity.

"Mr. Worth," said Missy. "And he asks if I will go for a drive with him this afternoon."

"This afternoon? That is very short notice, Missy," said her sister.

"Indeed, I don't know if it would be proper to accept," said Dillie. "You don't want to appear too fast."

Missy looked out the window where the sun was shining.

"He should have asked for tomorrow, or the next day," said Angelica.

"Well, he didn't," replied Missy sensibly. "And I can think of nothing I would rather do this afternoon than go for a drive. I will send him a note of acceptance."

In the back of her mind lurked the wayward gratification that Garrett didn't like Mr. Worth very much and would probably be quite vexed that she was out driving with the man. *So much the better!* cooed a decidedly feminine voice from the depths of her mind.

"You know, Sophie, you are one of the most charming women of my acquaintance," Garrett said, glancing at his passenger as he guided his pair through the crowded roadway leading to Rotten Row.

Sophie Beauclaire, an opera singer of dubious French antecedents, fluttered her long, dark lashes and whimpered, "But, *mon cheri*, have I not pleased you?"

"Well, of course you have. What man wouldn't be pleased by a beauty such as you, Sophie. But I've responsibilities now, what with my three wards living under my roof."

"Were they not under your roof last week when you came to me?" she asked with a pretty pout.

Garrett guided his horses into place behind a large, open landaulet carrying three ladies with two footmen hanging on to the rear. He groaned when he recognized the lady in the rear-facing seat—Ian's sister, Maggie. She nodded when she caught Garrett's eye. Her gaze shifted to Sophie; Garrett almost laughed as he watched her expression change to indignation. Then he frowned.

Perhaps he shouldn't have brought Sophie to Hyde Park to tell her good-bye. Perhaps he should have taken her on an intimate picnic in the country, away from prying eyes. Oh, Maggie wouldn't hold it against him, but there might be others.

"Who is that girl with Mr. Worth, Garrett?" asked Sophie brightly, who had been smiling at each gentleman as they passed by. "I think she is waving to you."

"What the deuce," he breathed, pulling his horses to a standstill and glaring at Worth's passing carriage.

"Hello, Garrett," said Missy, turning slightly to face him, but Fitzsimmons Worth whipped up his horses and passed too quickly for any other exchange.

Garrett would have turned his curricle if there had been enough room, but the crush of carriages prevented him from such a precipitous move.

"Just wait."

"What is wrong, Garrett? Who was that young lady?

Is she the reason you are leaving me?" asked the beautiful actress.

For Garrett, his surprise at finding Sophie by his side was a revelation, a dawning; he had completely forgotten her presence when he saw Missy riding beside that bounder Worth. What the devil was going on? What was happening to him? he wondered.

"Was she?" demanded Sophie, her French accent slipping.

"What? No, no. That is, in a way she is. That was one of my wards."

"Oh, so that's what it was," murmured Sophie, forgetting her accent completely.

"Yes, that's all. I think I can turn the curricle up here. Would you mind so very much if I took you home, my dear?" asked Garrett, already maneuvering his horses out of line.

"Of course not," said the girl. What choice did she have? Her chance of becoming the handsome Sir Garrett's mistress was dissolving into ashes even as they spoke.

Garrett dropped Sophie off at the house where she shared rented rooms with another fledgling actress. He drove away without a backward glance.

He couldn't wait until he could talk some sense into Missy. She had no idea the kind of person Fitzsimmons Worth really was. She had thought to annoy him, and she had, but he had to put a stop to it.

Garrett rounded the corner into Portman Square just as Worth pulled away from his door. Garrett eased back on the ribbons, stopping his cattle for a moment before turning them and following Worth.

His quarry next stopped at Weston's shop, and Garrett hopped down and followed him inside, leaving his tiger to walk his horses.

"Is Mr. Worth here?" asked Garrett when he didn't see his target.

"Yes, sir. He's gone to the back to be fitted for a coat."

Garrett handed the clerk his card, saying, "Would you be so good as to inquire if I might have a word?"

"Of course, Sir Garrett," said the clerk, accepting the coin Garrett tossed to him. He returned after a moment and signaled to Garrett to follow him.

"Good afternoon, Wyndridge," said Worth, turning this way and that to see himself in the mirrors. "I like it, but I still think the sleeves are a trifle short."

"Of course, sir. I'll have that fixed for you," said the clerk, helping to ease his client out of the fitted coat and into his old one.

Worth tugged at his cravat and asked over his shoulder, "What can I do for you, Wyndridge?"

"Do? You can quit chasing after my ward, that's what," said Garrett, his voice low so that no one could overhear their conversation.

"Now, why would a guardian request such a thing? Here am I, well able to provide for a wife, and you want me to stay away from your ward? That's a bit peculiar, wouldn't you say?"

"You know why, Worth. You and I have never gotten along, or do I need to remind you of that?"

"I have never understood that either, Wyndridge. Perhaps you would care to tell me why you feel this unwarranted animosity toward me."

"Unwarranted, ha! I seem to recall it began the first time our paths crossed back at school," drawled Garrett.

"My, my, but you do have a long memory. Surely you realize it was just a boyish prank; you soon proved to everyone that you weren't the sort to cheat on an examination," said Worth with a nasty laugh.

"And you soon proved that you were," said Garrett. "Then there was the time you ruined that girl, just because you thought I was courting her."

"Hardly, my dear fellow. And really, you should thank me. She was a nobody."

"I don't think her parents thought that. And you know there's more to it than all that."

"Then I beg your forgiveness, old man. After all, it wouldn't do to have bad blood in the family, now would it?"

"Worth," said Garrett, stepping closer and looking his opponent in the eye, "I'll see you rot in hell before I allow my ward to marry you." He turned on his heel and stalked out of the room, feeling much better by the time he had put several miles between him and his old enemy.

Garrett thought about returning to the house and speaking to Missy, but he simply didn't feel like coming to cuffs with her. Instead, he took the coward's way out and drove to his club, passing the remainder of the afternoon and the evening in the convivial company of his friends.

Missy attended two balls and a musicale that evening; by pure strength of will, her thoughts seldom strayed to Garrett. By the end of the night, she was even managing to not look up every time a door opened. Her guardian was no doubt passing his time with that bit of muslin, as Mr. Worth had termed her.

Missy tried not to allow this thought to plague her, but she had little success, for it haunted her dreams if not her well-disciplined consciousness.

Wednesday morning, Missy arose at ten o'clock and dressed hurriedly in her old gold riding habit. On her way to the stables, she went through the kitchens, begging a carrot from the cook for Tucker.

"Good morning, Lady Miss," said Putty, tugging at his cap.

"Good morning, Putty. How are you doing this morning?"

"Fine, miss. It does feel like it's goin' t' rain, though," said the giant servant, cupping his hands for Missy to mount.

"Oh, is your arm bothering you again?"

"Just this elbow, miss. It always draws up like when it's coming fer a storm."

"I will ask my sister to make up a poultice or something for you," said Missy. "She is very clever about such things."

"How is Miss Felicity?" asked the giant, swinging easily onto his horse's back, his legs hanging down even though the animal's back was almost as broad as a dray horse is.

"Oh, she is fine. We are all excited because we are to go to Almack's tonight. It is quite an honor to receive tickets, I believe."

"Even I knows that, miss," said Putty, setting his horse's nose just to the right of Tucker's rump to shield his mistress from any fast-moving vehicles as they entered the road.

"Good morning, Missy," said Garrett, meeting them as they left Portman Square behind.

"Good morning, Garrett," said Missy coolly, wishing she could have continued as she was with only the easygoing Putty for escort.

But Garrett turned his big gelding, saying, "Putty, why don't you go back to the stables? I'll escort Miss Lambert."

"Yes, sir," said Putty, turning the huge horse and heading back the way they had come.

Garrett studied the changing emotions flitting across Missy's face as she watched Putty disappear from sight. Then she met his gaze and pasted a smile on her face.

"Shall we?" he asked, allowing her to lead the way.

"I was fine with Putty, Garrett. You needn't have put yourself out on my account."

"I wasn't, Missy. I wanted to talk to you anyway."

He watched her profile change as her jaw became set in mulish lines. The sun glinted off her dark hair, the reddish strands sparkling like fire.

"What did you wish to speak to me about?" asked Missy, her tones clipped and prickly.

Garrett smiled. He didn't wish to spoil this idyllic ride by bringing up his old enemy's name, a topic which was sure to spark resentment in both of them.

"I just wanted to know if you and Felicity have everything you need," he lied.

"We . . . I . . . that is, yes, thank you. We have everything we need and then some, Garrett. You have been most generous," replied Missy.

"And everyone has been kind to you?"

"Very much so. I must admit, I did not expect to enjoy myself while here, but it is difficult not to when Felicity is so clearly in her element. I'm so happy she has, as they say, taken."

"I had no doubt. I am rather surprised that Angelica has her own entourage of beaux. When she first arrived, well, I was afraid she was a little too . . ."

"Spoiled?" asked Missy, her eyes meeting Garrett's. They laughed, enjoying this mutual understanding.

Garrett added, "Yes, Angelica is a bit spoiled, but I think she has learned from your sister's sweet disposition that one can catch more flies with honey."

"I agree, but in Felicity's case, being congenial is what she is."

"True, but it hasn't hurt Angelica to practice some of that consideration. She was quite a handful that week before you arrived," said Garrett, falling silent when this topic was exhausted.

What he really wanted to know, really wanted to ask, was if Missy was happy. He wanted to know if being with Worth that afternoon had been necessary to that happiness, or if she cared at all about the man. Most of all, he realized with a start, had she forgiven him for taking her home from her, for bringing her to London?

But he couldn't ask those things. He didn't dare.

They were turning into the stable yard before Missy finally found her tongue. She had been unable to come up with a topic of conversation that she thought she could sustain beyond a single sentence.

Finally, she asked, "So you are going to Almack's with us tonight?"

"Of course. I wouldn't miss it," said Garrett, smiling down at her. Looking into those expressive dark eyes, he added impulsively, "And I have something for you to wear."

"For me? But I already have a gown," said Missy.

"I know that. A sapphire blue gown, yes?" he asked. Missy nodded, and Garrett continued smoothly, "My mother had a sapphire necklace, a single teardrop stone on a chain encrusted with diamonds. I thought you might like to borrow it."

"Why, that would be lovely. Thank you, Garrett," said Missy, kicking free of the stirrups and sliding to the ground unaided.

"Until tonight," said Garrett, waving to her as she hurried toward the house.

A knock on the door dragged Missy's attention away from the long cheval glass where she had been captivated by her surprising image.

"Dulcie, you're a wonder," she said again as the pleased maid answered the door. "How in the world did you manage to tame this wild mane of mine? Every curl in place and behaving."

Garrett entered the room, his broad shoulders blocking the light from the hallway. Missy flushed, wondering if he had heard her words.

"Whatever she did, you look wonderful," he said, and she turned a darker shade of pink.

Missy stepped forward, but he stayed her with a raised hand, saying, "I'm sorry I am late bringing this to you." He crossed the room and handed her a flat velvet box.

"Oh, yes, the necklace. I had almost forgotten," lied Missy, opening the box. In truth, she thought he had forgotten or perhaps changed his mind. The diamonds in the chain winked at her as she lifted the choker from its velvet bed.

"I think this is the most beautiful thing I have ever seen, Garrett. Are you certain you want me to wear it?" she breathed.

Garrett held the box while Missy turned back to the mirror, her hands shaking as she held the necklace in place and tried to fasten the catch.

"Oh, dear," she said, as it slid to the floor.

"Allow me," said Garrett, retrieving the necklace and placing it around her neck. He fastened it easily, but his touch sent a shiver the length of her spine. Neither moved. She wanted to raise her head to meet his eyes in the mirror's reflection, but she didn't dare; he would detect her uncertainty, and she didn't want to give him access to her heart.

"Missy?" he managed finally.

His tone invited her to lean into the circle of his arms. She couldn't, of course. She wouldn't, but the temptation was almost overwhelming.

Clearing her throat, Missy fixed a bright smile on her face and moved away from the full-length glass. Walking stiffly to the small dressing table, she leaned down to pretend an intense study of each small diamond. The single sapphire settled against her breasts, feeling cold against her skin.

"Thank you, Garrett. I will look after it well," she said, not looking up.

Garrett took his cue and excused himself, hurrying

out of the room. Missy sank onto the bench, staring at her reflection.

"Oh, miss, you do look a fair treat," said Dulcie, appearing from nowhere.

"Only because you have worked miracles," said Missy, shaking off her pensiveness. After all, she was to attend Almack's in an hour. She was one of the lucky ones. Less fortunate ladies went into declines for want of vouchers to Almack's hallowed hall.

So why in the world did she have the absurd desire to laugh hysterically?

The rooms that housed Almack's were not spectacular, but the ladies were duly impressed by the company gathered there. And though they may not have realized it, the company, at least the males present, were quite impressed with what they saw when Garrett, resplendent in his new knee breeches, ushered his wards inside.

Missy was a dark-haired beauty in her sapphire blue gown, the diamond chain and heavy sapphire drawing all eyes to her creamy breasts. Felicity, with her golden blond hair, and Angelica, with her silvery blond, wore pastel gowns that made their complexions shine. Both of them wore single strands of pearls, gifts from Garrett, that befitted their youth. Even Dillie wore a new gown, a pale purple with a matching turban.

As they waited their turn to be announced, Missy whispered to Felicity, "Now I can die happy."

"Sh! Someone will hear you, Missy!" hissed her sister in return, but she smiled all the same.

As soon as they entered the hall, Garrett took each of their dance cards and wrote his name in one place. If he lingered overlong on Missy's, he managed to control any impulse to write his name twice and handed it back to her with a silent smile.

Then he turned to Dillie, saying, "Will you do me the honor of dancing the boulanger when it begins in a few moments?"

"Oh, Garrett, you don't want to dance with an old thing like me," she protested, turning a pleased pink all the same.

"Why, Dillie, I have seen you put the young ladies to shame with your grace and enthusiasm. Surely you won't deny me the privilege?"

Dillie giggled and nodded. "Very well, Garrett, my dear boy. If you insist, but first I must see to it that my girls are partnered properly."

"Only look around," said Garrett. "They all have gentlemen vying for the privilege of a dance. You may enjoy yourself with impunity, my dear lady."

Dillie held out her hand, and they took their place. From her place in the set, Missy smiled approvingly at Garrett. Then she turned her attention on her partner, an older gentleman with thinning hair and a hook nose.

"You know, Dillie," Garrett said, "I have been meaning to tell you what a splendid job you are doing with the girls."

"How nice of you to say so, but I truly think you should compliment the girls themselves. I have never known three more well-behaved young ladies. And they are all so sweet."

"Even Angelica?" asked Garrett in his teasing way.

"Yes, even Angelica. I think she just needed a little companionship. Felicity is good for her, but she is also good for Felicity. Missy is not as keen to discuss fashion and such as her sister, so Angelica is someone for Felicity to talk to."

"You're very observant," said Garrett. "I really hadn't thought about that. You're right, of course. I suppose Missy has always loved being outside and riding. Felicity is more of a homebody."

"True, but they are both dears. Especially Missy, but I think you have noticed that, haven't you?" said Dillie.

Garrett put on his stern face and said, "I don't know what you mean." Fortunately for him, the steps of the dance separated them, and Dillie, who never shied away from forthright speech, didn't have a chance to explain to him exactly what she meant.

Garrett set himself to please each of his partners. Halfway through the evening, he thought he had danced with every young lady present. The next dance was to be a waltz, and he had signed Missy's card for it. He waited anxiously for the music to end so he could join her.

The quadrille ended, and Princess Lieven tapped him on the shoulder, cooing, "Sir Garrett, my dear sir. You must be exhausted. But could you possibly have the energy to waltz with me?"

"Well, I'm afraid I have already signed my ward's card, Your Highness."

Missy, who had walked up in time to catch most of the exchange, said hurriedly, "Please allow me to give up my place for you, Your Highness. It is the least I can do since you allowed my sister and me to attend."

"No, no, my dear. I wouldn't wish to disappoint your, uh, guardian," said the princess. "Enjoy yourself, Sir Garrett."

"Thank you, Your Highness," he replied, taking Missy's arm none too gently. "You know, Missy, if you don't wish to waltz with me, you need only tell me, not try to foist me off on someone else."

The injustice of his accusation made Missy grind her teeth, but the music had begun and his hold on her wouldn't allow her to escape. She remained silent for the first few minutes.

Finally, Garrett relented. "I suppose that was poorly done of me, Missy."

"Yes."

"It just seemed to me you were a little too eager to be rid of me, and I thought we had become friends."

"So did I."

Garrett tightened his hold on her, and they made a few dizzying twirls.

"Forgive me now?" he asked, grinning down at her.

It required some effort, but Missy said nothing.

"You asked for it," murmured Garrett, whispering in her ear.

He began to lead her through the other dancers, somehow missing every couple as they progressed in a wild, twisting jaunt.

Laughing and breathless, Garrett finally slowed their pace.

"I cry peace," she managed.

"You're not mad anymore for my ham-fisted behavior?"

"No, I'm not mad. I really wasn't that angry to begin with, Garrett. It is just so aggravating when you jump to conclusions."

"Mea culpa. A lifelong fault, I fear. It is good to know you are so forgiving, my dear," he added.

"Just do not try my patience too far, sir," she warned with a wicked giggle. "Really, Garrett, I would have forgiven you a great deal for what you did for Dillie. I thought she would swoon, she was so pleased."

"Well, why shouldn't she dance? She may not be a girl anymore, but she is not in the grave. And I notice she has had several other offers since then, in particular Admiral Tupperman. I think I scent orange blossoms there."

"Do you really think so? Oh, that would be marvelous. She deserves some happiness. She is such a dear."

"She's not the only one," said Garrett, looking at her pointedly.

Missy's eyes flew to his face, but he was smiling in that way meant to charm the ladies. She dropped her gaze; so it was only his way of flirting. Looking up again, she forced herself to return his empty smile, but she didn't look in his eyes.

Garrett thought perhaps the twirling had made him dizzy. Why else would he have said such an outrageous thing? It was the sort of compliment one paid to a lady that meant absolutely nothing. It was also the sort one said, and meant, when you loved her.

* * *

Garrett awoke the next morning with a groan. Hoisting himself up to a sitting position, he realized first that he was not in his comfortable feather bed. He was in his study, on the old leather sofa, and though it was quite comfortable for a short doze, it was not *convenable* for a full night of sleep. Every muscle ached.

"Good morning, Garrett," said Ian Emery, entering the room and dropping onto the sofa. He leaned forward and poured two cups of hot coffee.

"That butler of yours is priceless, Garrett. Turtle always knows when you're going to wake up. Always knows when to bring the coffee," observed Ian.

"Oh, shaddup and hand me a cup. What brings you out so demmed early this morning?"

"I have to go down to my estate for a day or so, and I wondered if you might like to go with me. Thought maybe you could do with a day away from petticoat rule," said Ian, investigating what lay beneath the covered cloth on the silver tray and heaving a sigh of pleasure when he found his favorite scones.

"Why the devil would I want to ride for three hours only to turn around and come back?" grumbled Garrett.

"I suppose you don't. I just thought I would ask. I mean, from the rumors I hear, you were positively danced off your feet at Almack's last night. You've got more hopeful mamas after you than I ever did!" laughed his friend. "Why, you'll hardly be able to show your face in the street without tripping over some fainting damsel falling into your arms."

"You're exaggerating, Ian," said Garrett, the sleep finally leaving him as he sipped the hot liquid.

"If you say so, but I went to the club for breakfast, and there is already talk. It seems they all find you charming and . . . let's see, I think the word used was amenable."

Garrett choked on his coffee, and Ian obligingly pounded his back while he sputtered and spewed.

"Amenable! I'll show them amenable. I'll not have some blasted chit lead me around by the nose. Give me half an hour to shave and dress, and I'll be down, ready to go."

"Happy to, old chap. I'll just stay here with my scones," said Ian, settling in to wait.

Five minutes later, there was a scratching at the door, and Felicity peeked inside. Her eyes widened when she saw Ian.

"I beg your pardon, Mr. Emery. I thought to have a word with Cousin Garrett."

Hastily brushing crumbs off his waistcoat, Ian rose and sketched a casual bow.

"He should be back down in a few moments, Miss Felicity, if you would care to wait."

"I . . . suppose so," she replied, coming in and settling in beside him.

"Garrett and I are going to visit my estate for the next day or two. I have one or two matters I must attend to, and Garrett agreed to accompany me."

"Where is your estate, Mr. Emery?"

"North of London. A three-hour ride. It is not so very large, but it is quite prosperous," he said.

"That's nice," murmured Felicity, wondering if she would ever find her tongue. In a shaky voice, she said, "Please, Mr. Emery, do sit down again. I am like to get a stiff neck looking up at you."

Ian resumed his seat, wishing the sofa would grow in length. Even her perfume was calculated to entice him, he thought, breathing deeply.

"That's a nice scent you have on, Miss Felicity," he said, suddenly tongue-tied, sounding like an untried schoolboy instead of a rake.

"Oh, I don't wear scent," she confided with a smile. "It's the French soap I bathe with," she added, never realizing the pictures her childish disclosure sent to her listener.

Ian frowned. Really, the girl was too naive. She should be instructed in how to converse with a gentleman. And here she was, alone with a rogue like him. What were they thinking, turning such an innocent loose without proper supervision? Well, someone had to explain to her how to go on. He supposed he would have to take over.

"My dear child," he began.

"I am not a child, Mr. Emery. I know everyone thinks of me in that way, but truly, I am quite mature for my eighteen years. And I will be nineteen next month," said Felicity.

"But, Felicity . . . Miss Felicity . . . you really shouldn't be telling a man about the soap you use to, uh, that is—"

"To bathe? Why ever not? Doesn't everyone bathe?" she asked, beginning to enjoy herself.

"Now, you know what I mean," said Ian, his eyes narrowing as he studied her wide-eyed expression that never wavered. "Why, you minx!" he said, chuckling.

"I told you I was not such a child as you have been led to believe. You know, Mr. Emery, that for the past five years I have managed our household. Oh, I grant you, I have an excellent housekeeper, but I kept the books and planned all the meals. What is more—and I know this will shock you—I earned money by sewing and making lace trimming for the dressmaker in our village."

"I had no idea you were so enterprising," said Ian Emery, a new admiration lighting his pale blue eyes.

"Oh, I am, Mr. Emery. At least, I was before. Since coming to London, I have let everyone tell me what to do and how to behave, and I am finding it rather confining," said Felicity, never dropping her eyes, but watching him boldly.

"Confining? In what way?" asked Ian, leaning closer.

"I . . . I . . ." But she had lost her nerve and would have pulled back. "Well, never mind that, but as for those scones you like so very much, you should just taste mine. They positively melt in your mouth!" she added proudly.

Ian, however, threw caution to the wind and kissed her, softly and gently. Smiling, Felicity pulled away to study his face. She must have liked the warmth in his eyes, for she leaned forward again, melting against him this time for a proper kiss.

When Garrett entered the room a few minutes later, they were conversing about the weather and sipping from their coffee cups.

Six

"Now, girls, I have received an exciting invitation for us. I wasn't sure if I should accept, but I think it will be perfectly suitable."

"What is it, Dillie?" asked Angelica, scenting an adventure.

"Lady Ridgemar is giving a masked ball," breathed the older woman, her cheeks as flushed as Missy's had been only a moment before. "The admiral told me he would be going, and he offered to escort us since Cousin Garrett is away for the night."

"A masquerade," breathed Angelica. Then she grinned, looking at Felicity and Missy in turn, and added, "What fun! We must create some sort of costumes. I wonder if there is anything in the attics."

"I doubt it," said Missy. "My father rented out this house for years. I daresay the tenants will have cleaned everything out when they vacated the house."

"But we can look and see," said Felicity, hopping up to join Angelica at the door.

"Yes, Missy. Let's go upstairs and see if there is anything we can use," said Dillie. "I remember one masked ball I attended many years ago. It was so much fun!"

"Oh, very well. Who knows? We might find a treasure chest," said Missy, beginning to catch their enthusiasm.

In the end, the ladies found little to use and were forced to beg Turtle and Anderson, whose nose was out of joint that Garrett had left him behind, for suggestions. They rummaged through a little-used storage closet in the servants' wing and found a number of vital accessories. The ladies chose what they wanted to use and scurried to their rooms, deciding to surprise each other with their costumes. The day passed quickly, and before they knew it, Admiral Tupperman had arrived for dinner.

Missy put the final touches on her costume, setting her hat at a jaunty angle. She grinned at her reflection. For the first time since coming to London, she felt completely at home in her clothes, she reflected. The "man" staring back at her was as familiar as an old friend. The country smock and breeches were her own, the same ones she wore when working around the stables. The hat, a wide-brimmed straw, had been unearthed in the mews by Putty, along with the sturdy shoes. She supposed one of the stableboys was going about in his bare feet, but she needed the shoes; her old boots would never do for a ball, even if they did complement the rest of her ensemble.

Tipping her hat to her image, she hurried out the door and down the stairs where the others were waiting to go in to dinner.

The admiral was dressed in his usual old-fashioned knee breeches and a satin coat; he carried a black silk domino and several black masks dangled from his fingers. Dillie was dressed as a pirate. Missy blinked twice before she remembered to close her mouth. The admiral didn't notice; he was too busy bowing over Dillie's hand, kissing it fervently.

"My dear, you look divine," leered the old reprobate.

"Dear Tupper, I vow you are a rascal," said Dillie, simpering like a schoolgirl.

"Oh, Missy, you haven't even dressed up," exclaimed Felicity, who was accustomed to seeing her sister dressed like a countryman at home.

"Not dressed up?" said Angelica. "I think you look wonderful! With a mask, no one will guess your identity. And I think it daring of you to dress like a man."

"Indeed, you look charming, m'dear," said the admiral. "And I brought extra masks for each of you."

"Thank you, Admiral."

"I shall be the luckiest man there tonight, having all of you beauties in my company," said the old man, offering an arm to both Missy and Dillie and leading them into the dining room.

Felicity and Angelica linked arms and followed.

"You look ravishing, my dear," whispered Angelica, her voice low and masculine. "Quite the Grecian goddess."

"And you, kind sir, look wonderful as a fairy princess," laughed Felicity, playing her role as coquette to perfection.

Giggling, they took their seats around the table, insisting that the admiral sit at the head in Garrett's absence. It was a merry meal, though the girls drank lemonade instead of wine, Dillie warning them that they must keep their wits about them at a masquerade.

When they arrived at Lord and Lady Ridgemar's Richmond mansion just outside London, Missy peered out the window for a moment before sitting back and commenting, "It seems the ball will be quite a crush, Dillie. I had no idea so many would attend."

"It's not like those select balls you have attended so far, my dear. That is why I said you must keep your wits about you. But you'll have a rollicking good time," said Dillie, rapping the admiral on his arm smartly when he gave her a leering wink.

"But it is perfectly proper for us to be here," said Missy dubiously.

"Of course it is," injected Angelica. "You have only to look at the elegant carriages to realize that only *la crème de la crème* of Society will be here tonight."

"I suppose," said Missy slowly.

"Ian . . . that is, Mr. Emery . . . mentioned that he would be here," said Felicity, keeping her voice even and calm.

"And I'll be here to keep an eye on all my girls," said the admiral, his bluff announcement negated by the smirk he was bestowing on Dillie.

The old spinster's blush made Missy giggle; she told herself she was only being missish, and vowed to relax and enjoy the masquerade.

They had finally arrived at the door, and a footman, dressed like a galley slave, opened the carriage door and helped the ladies descend. When they had climbed the stairs to the receiving line, there were more footmen; these were armed with huge palm branches which they wafted back and forth to cool the guests who were waiting to greet their host and hostess.

"Delightful," pronounced Dillie.

"Exotic," said Angelica.

"Foolish," muttered Missy. She stepped forward and made her curtsy, taking the ends of her smock and extending them outward like the skirts of a gown.

"Charming girl," murmured Lord Ridgemar.

"Please, my dear, enjoy yourself. This is like to be the entertainment of the year," said Lady Ridgemar.

"I'm sure it will be," said Missy before moving forward and joining her sister on the steps above the sunken ballroom where masked revelers were already enjoying a lively waltz.

"Isn't it exciting?" breathed Felicity, her blue eyes flashing between the slits of her white mask.

She wore a white gown over which she had draped a white sheet, giving her the look of a Grecian maiden. Her blond hair was piled high on her head, with ringlets dangling around one ear. Missy looked down at her own garb and grimaced. She should have chosen something more feminine. Beside Felicity, no one would give her a second glance.

Over the last strains of the waltz, Missy heard creaking and turned to find a knight in full armor bowing before her.

"My lady, would you do me the honor of the next dance?" asked the knight, his eyes on her stockinged legs rather than her face.

Missy thought about giving him a setdown, but she

remembered her pledge to enjoy herself and said, "It would be my pleasure, good knight."

She turned to find Felicity accepting the invitation of a stuttering young man with humped shoulders and a thatch of unruly hair. With a little wave, Felicity and her youthful swain took their places in the quadrille. Missy and the knight followed, joining the next square.

As the dance progressed, the creaking of her partner's armor increased with each step, each turn, until finally he whispered an embarrassed, "Excuse me," and fled, leaving Missy standing awkwardly by herself. But this was a masked ball and the rules were flexible, to be sure. A gentleman in a black domino stepped forward from the edge of the ballroom and took the knight's place.

When the steps of the dance brought them together, he murmured, "How fortunate for me your knight was rusting away. I do hope you'll agree to sup with me, my dear, for having saved the day."

Missy laughed. "Not quite the tale of rescuing damsels in distress."

"But surely I read distress in your eyes when the cur deserted you."

"Distress, sir, but it wasn't quite like saving me from a dragon," said Missy, eyeing her rescuer. She knew this man; she couldn't place him yet, but she was certain she had met him before.

The steps of the dance separated them, and when they met again, the man placed his hand over his heart in a dramatic gesture and announced grandly, "Only show me a dragon, fair damsel, and I will gladly slay him."

Missy laughed; shaking her head, she whispered, "You, Mr. Worth, should have gone on the stage. I think you would have gone far."

"But you have guessed my identity, fair maiden," he said with a groan. Then, just before they parted once more, he whispered, "And I have guessed yours, but I shan't tell a soul, for fear that guardian of yours will descend on me and demand satisfaction."

"Oh? I thought you said you would slay my dragons for me," said Missy, amazed at her outrageousness.

Through the slits of his black mask, she saw his eyes narrow dangerously, and a shiver shook her body. The music ended with a crescendo, and the couples curtsyed and bowed to each other.

"I didn't realize he was your dragon," he said, his mouth so close to her ear that Missy could feel the warmth of his breath. Again she shivered and drew back, forcing herself to smile.

"La, sir, you do say the silliest things," she drawled, backing away from him.

Turning, she fled, her eyes darting this way and that, looking for Dillie and the admiral. They were nowhere to be seen. So much for counting on his protection this evening, Missy thought resentfully. Judging from the disgraceful leers they had been casting at each other, they had probably found some secluded spot to be alone.

That was all well and good for them, but it left Missy very much in charge of her sister and of Angelica. She returned to the ballroom as the waltz was ending. Finding a spot behind a large potted fern, Missy scanned the couples now filling the dance floor in preparation for the next set. She breathed a sigh of relief. There was Angelica in her guise as a fairy princess; at least she was easy to spot with her ridiculously high silver-tinsel crown. And there was Felicity, waiting patiently for the music to begin, her partner this time a dark-haired Zeus.

Missy frowned as another waltz began. It was unusual to have two waltzes so close together.

"It is by far the best way to get to know one's partner, said Mr. Worth, appearing by her side. Missy shrugged but said nothing, hoping to depress his intentions.

"It is also the preferred dance of most of the gentlemen present," he added. "Do you waltz, Miss Lambert?"

"Not with the same gentleman I just partnered in the quadrille, sir," she replied tartly.

He laughed. "You are a proper young lady, Miss Lambert. I admire that in a, uh, countryman."

Missy couldn't stop herself from smiling, feeling at ease with him once again. As long as he recognized her, she thought, she would put him to good use.

"Who is that Zeus my sister is dancing with, Mr. Worth?"

"That, I believe, is Ridgemar's eldest. A frightfully dull young man who, if one is to credit the rumors, prefers the schoolroom to the ballroom."

"If you were my brother, would you consider him a suitable partner for Felicity?"

"If I were your brother, my dear Miss Lambert, I would have hauled both of you home by now."

Frowning, Missy turned on him. "Whatever do you mean by that, sir?"

"Only that a masked ball is hardly the place for

proper young ladies. Oh, I grant you that someone as mature as you are, Miss Lambert, is quite safe attending this evening's soiree, but young innocents such as your sister, and even the, shall we be charitable and say, strong-willed Miss Wyndridge are risking their reputations by attending this ball."

"Really? I had no idea!" exclaimed Missy, starting forward only to be pulled back behind the fern. "Let me go, Mr. Worth! I must get my sister and cousin and go home!"

"Not until the waltz is over, my dear girl. To act so precipitously would only ensure their downfall. No, they will be fine as long as they leave before the unmasking. That way, tomorrow when the gossips are dissecting the masquerade, no one can say for certain who attended the ball."

Missy nodded, giving him a rueful smile. "You are very kind, sir, to take an interest in the reputations of strangers."

"Not strangers, Miss Lambert. At least, not you and I," he continued, taking her hand and lifting it to his lips.

The music stopped suddenly. A rapid fanfare of trumpets made everyone turn to the dais where Lady Ridgemar stood, flanked by two of her "galley slaves."

"Ladies and gentlemen, let us add a little spice to this evening. For the next fifteen minutes, the musicians will stop and start a waltz at irregular intervals. Each time the music stops, you must seek a new partner, one you haven't had before. There is only one trick to this, however. Like the children's game of musical chairs, I will be taking away several gentlemen each time the music stops, and the ladies without a partner must withdraw. The last couple left on the dance floor will lead us in to supper and will lead us in the unmasking."

A round of applause followed the announcement. Lady Ridgemar turned and gave the signal to the musicians to begin.

Before Missy knew what was happening, Mr. Worth had led her onto the floor and swept her into his arms. He didn't waltz as well as Garrett did; but then, she was learning not to compare other men to her guardian.

The music stopped; Missy found herself partnering Felicity's Zeus. They swirled past a tall, red-haired gentleman who could only be Ian Emery; he held tightly to his partner, a lady in a filmy gown that clung to her body the way she was clinging to Mr. Emery. The music stopped; Ian's partner giggled loudly as he kissed her, refusing to let her go. The music began again, with the two of them still partners.

Again the music stopped. This time, Missy thanked her partner and left the floor before some other gentleman could claim her. Ian was still wrestling with his friend, only releasing her when she squealed, clinging to another gentleman in a disgraceful manner.

Laughing, Ian turned and claimed another partner—Felicity. Missy watched in horror as Felicity raised her hand to slap his face. He reeled when the blow touched home, his eyes flashing with anger. With a loud sob, Felicity pivoted and ran, Missy following on her heels.

Missy returned shortly to the ballroom and hauled Angelica away. It took her a full half hour to locate

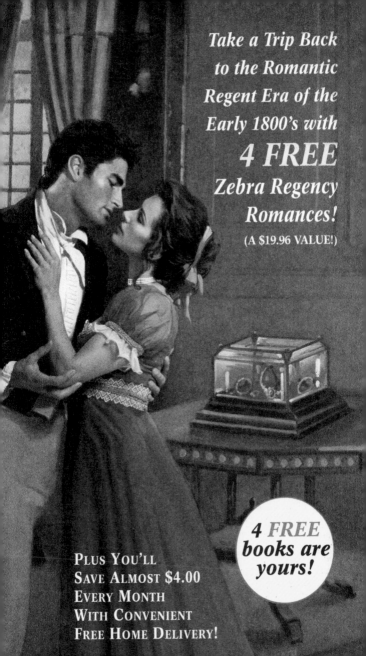

We'd Like to Invite You to Subscribe to Zebra's Regency Romance Book Club an Give You a Gift of 4 Free Books as Your Introduction! (Worth $19.96!)

If you're a Regency lover, imagine the joy of getting **4 FREE Zebra Regency Romances** and then the chance to have th lovely stories delivered to your home each month at the lowest prices available! Well, that's our offer to you and here's how you benefit by becoming a Regency Romance subscriber:

- **4 FREE** Introductory Regency Romances are delivered to your doors
- 4 BRAND NEW Regencies are then delivered each month (usually befo they're available in bookstores)
- Subscribers save almost $4.00 every month
- Home delivery is always **FREE**
- You also receive a **FREE** monthly newsletter, *Zebra/Pinnacle Roman News* which features author profiles, contests, subscriber benefits, b previews and more
- No risks or obligations...in other words you can cancel whenever yo wish with no questions asked

Join the thousands of readers who enjoy the savings and convenience offered to Regency Romance subscribers. After your initial introductory shipment, you receive 4 brand-new Zebra Regency Romances each month to examine for 10 days Then, if you decide to keep the books, you'll pay the preferred subscriber's price of just $4.00 per title. That's only $16.00 for all 4 books and there's never an extra charge for shipping and handling.

It's a no-lose proposition, so return the FREE BOOK CERTIFICATE today!

Say Yes to 4 Free Books!

Complete and return the order card to receive this
$19.96 value, ABSOLUTELY FREE!

If the certificate is missing below, write to:
Zebra Home Subscription Service, Inc.,
P.O. Box 5214, Clifton, New Jersey 07015-5214
or call TOLL-FREE 1-888-345-BOOK
Visit our website at www.kensingtonbooks.com.

FREE BOOK CERTIFICATE

YES! Please rush me 4 Zebra Regency Romances without cost or obligation. I understand that each month thereafter I will be able to preview 4 brand-new Regency Romances FREE for 10 days. Then, if I should decide to keep them, I will pay the money-saving preferred subscriber's price of just $16.00 for all 4...that's a savings of almost $4 off the publisher's price with no additional charge for shipping and handling. I may return any shipment within 10 days and owe nothing, and I may cancel this subscription at any time. My 4 FREE books will be mine to keep in any case.

Name _____

Address _____ Apt. _____

City _____ State _____ Zip _____

Telephone ( ) _____

Signature _____ RN060A
(If under 18, parent or guardian must sign.)

Terms and prices subject to change. Orders subject to acceptance by Zebra Home Subscription Service, Inc. Offer valid in U.S. only.

PLACE
STAMP
HERE

llllmllmllllmllllmllmlllllmllmlllllmllmlllmlllml

REGENCY ROMANCE BOOK CLUB
Zebra Home Subscription Service, Inc.
P.O. Box 5214
Clifton NJ 07015-5214

Dillie and the admiral so they could leave. The un-masking was taking place; they could hear the excla-mations of delight and astonishment. Even as the carriage pulled away, Felicity peered back, her tear-streaked face causing Missy to breathe a silent curse for Ian Emery.

When they arrived home, the front parlor was ablaze with candlelight. Dillie pulled her eye patch off and placed it in her reticule, saying, "I believe Cousin Garrett must have come home early."

Missy sat up straighter, looking from one occupant of the coach to the other. In tones that brooked no argument, she announced, "We have done nothing wrong. If Cousin Garrett chooses to see things differ-ently, that is his problem. We will all stick together, understood?"

They managed to shake off their hangdog expres-sions long enough to nod.

"Good," said Missy, leading the way up the steps and into the house.

Garrett, wearing breeches and a dressing gown and sporting a day's growth of beard, stood in the hall, watching the ragamuffin band enter—the pirate and her admiral, the fairy princess, the bleary-eyed Greek goddess, and lastly, the most beautiful countryman he had ever seen. It took all his effort not to laugh out loud at the way they glanced at him, one by one, as ill at ease as schoolchildren caught in some scrape. Then his gaze met Missy's, and he knew who the ring-leader was by her defiant glare.

"I suppose you now know that a masquerade is not the proper place for young ladies," he said gravely.

"I'm sorry, Cousin Garrett," began Dillie.

"It was my fault, really, Sir Garrett," said the admiral.

"No, no, Tupper, it wasn't. The girls are in my charge."

"That is true, Dillie. I am very disappointed. I trusted you to guide my wards, to protect them."

"But we begged her to allow us to go," lied Angelica.

"Yes, Garrett. Please don't be mad at Dillie," said Felicity, sniffling slightly at the effort of speech.

"And you, Mystique, what have you to say?" asked Garrett, facing her squarely. It wouldn't do to back down from the challenge in her eyes.

"I say that you shouldn't call me Mystique, Sir Garrett! How many times must I remind you? *That's* what I say!" snapped Missy. She brushed past him and marched up the stairs to her room. Even from the hall, they could hear the door slam.

"We will discuss this in the morning. Good night, Admiral."

"What? Oh, yes, yes, my boy. Good night."

When the admiral had gone, Garrett said quietly, "I think it would be a good idea if you ladies stay in tomorrow night. There is no need to remind the gossips of your existence; they might put all of you and the masquerade together."

"But, Garrett . . ." began Angelica. Bowing her head, she fell silent beneath his raised brows.

"A word with you, Felicity," he said, stepping back and opening the door to the parlor.

"Of course," she whispered.

When she was seated on the sofa, he joined her and took her trembling hand in his.

"Ian came by just before you came home. He didn't realize you were even at the masquerade. He wanted me to apologize for him."

"He needn't have bothered," she replied, raising her chin proudly. "My eyes are fully opened now to the sort of man he is, and he is no gentleman," she finished.

Rising, she asked, "May I go to bed now?"

"Of course," replied Garrett, shaking his head sadly as he watched her regal progress to the door.

Garrett knew there would be a confrontation, and as an experienced soldier, he wanted to choose the battleground. Knowing Missy was always at her best on horseback, he chose to waylay her in the park the next morning, sending Putty back home so that Missy would be forced to remain in his company.

He hoped.

When Putty had ridden away, Missy said, "Whatever you wish to say to me, Garrett, you had best say it quickly, because I have no intention of wasting my time listening to a lecture that I have already given myself."

He opened his mouth, only to snap it closed again, frowning fiercely at her.

Then she laughed at him, saying, "I am sorry, Garrett, but if you could see your expression, you would laugh, too."

"I don't understand," he replied, still perplexed.

"I just decided to be honest with you and tell you how appalled I was at the goings-on we witnessed. I had no idea. I suppose I should have, but who would have thought people would behave so scandalously just because half their face was covered by a little mask!"

"What a relief," he said, grinning at her. "Wait a minute now. You're not just saying this so I will relent about this evening, are you?"

"Certainly not," she replied tartly. "I would never stoop to such trickery."

"Yes, well, I suppose I knew that." He chuckled and added, "Missy, you have no idea how I lay awake worrying about this morning. I know how you hate for me to tell you what to do. I just knew you were going to ring a peal over me for censuring you."

"And so I should, except that you are right. So we are friends again?" she asked.

"The very best of friends, Missy," said Garrett, leaning forward and shaking her hand. He held it a moment before asking quietly, "Were you very shocked?"

"Not too badly, except by Mr. Emery's behavior. I am so glad we steered Felicity away from him. I know she was shocked by his behavior—that is, after all, why she slapped him—but it is not as bad as if she had formed a tendre for him. And to be fair, Mr. Emery had no idea we were there. I daresay he would have behaved more circumspectly."

"Without a doubt; and he had hurried back to town just so he could attend the blasted thing. That will teach him!" agreed Garrett, enjoying this new relationship with Missy.

"Why, he probably would have helped me round up the girls, just like Mr. Worth did," said Missy without thinking.

"What the deuce was Worth doing there? Did he go with you, too?" demanded Garrett.

"No, Mr. Worth did not go with us, too!" rejoined Missy, her self-control fleeing. "He happened to recognize me, as I did him. He is the one who warned me that it was not proper for the younger girls to be there."

"And what of you? Did he tell you it was perfectly proper for a lady of your advanced age to flaunt herself in men's knee breeches and stockings?" He knew he was being harsh, but he simply couldn't control himself.

"That's not fair, Garrett!" she shouted.

He looked around to see if they were being observed. Thank heavens they had ridden all the way to Green Park instead of stopping at Hyde Park. It had fewer visitors at this early hour.

"Keep your voice down," he hissed. "You're going to make Tucker bolt."

Her teeth clenched, Missy ground out, "She doesn't do that anymore. I have trained her properly."

With that, she kicked the mare's sides, and she leapt forward and away, reaching a gallop in seconds, thundering across the green carpet of grass. Garrett caught them up at the entrance of the park, where Missy waited impatiently for him to escort her home.

At least she had not lost all sense of propriety, he thought grimly as they made their silent way back to the mews.

When they had dismounted, Missy hurried toward the house. Garrett turned to speak to Putty, but the vision of Missy's stormy retreat crowded his thoughts.

He turned to watch her disappear into the house; she had torn her hat from her head and was using it to beat an angry tattoo against her thigh.

Missy threw herself across the bed when she reached her room. Tears were streaming down her face, and she pitched the black and gold shako across the room without a thought. Never mind that it was her favorite hat; something or someone needed to pay for her anger, and Garrett was not within reach.

How could he be so insulting? And why on earth did he harbor such hatred for Worth? The man was not the monster Garrett painted him to be. Most of all, why did she even care what Garrett's opinions were—on any subject?

Missy rolled over and stared at the bed curtain ceiling of her bed. The dark blue satin fitted her mood precisely, enveloping her until she could not break free. Her frustration and anger threatened to consume her.

She had planned to make Sir Garrett Wyndridge rue the day he had been given guardianship over her. She had planned to try his patience, to aggravate him, and in general to rub him the wrong way every chance she had.

The last thing she had planned for, however, was to find herself distressed and confused by Garrett and her feelings for him. Where was the cold anger she had felt at having Garrett named as her guardian? Where was the anger that had consumed her when she read his letter summoning them to London? It

had been replaced by a rush of emotions that had
nothing to do with righteous indignation.

What was she going to do now?

"Missy? Oh, good, you are awake!"

Missy wiped away the last vestiges of tears and sat
up to face her cheerful sister.

"Since we are to remain quietly at home today, Dillie suggested I send for the modiste to bring my new
gowns for the final fittings. Shall I tell her to ask for
yours as well?" asked Felicity.

"What a good idea. I think I'll just get out of these
things and perhaps even have a bath. Let me know
when the modiste arrives," said Missy with false gai-
ety.

"I will!" called Felicity as she left the room.

Garrett sent word to his wards that he would be
dining with friends that evening, but he bade them
enjoy their quiet and advised them to take advantage
of the time to rest before rejoining the social whirl
the following night.

Dillie, mindful of having led her charges astray,
made every effort to be entertaining at supper. When
lemonade was served with the meal, she said, "Turtle,
bring us a bottle of the best champagne. We are of
a mind to enjoy ourselves this evening."

"Yes, Miss Dill," said the servant.

When he returned, he had a tray with glasses already filled with the golden liquid.

Dillie took one sip and declared, "Turtle, pour out
this watered-down rubbish immediately. And this
time, bring the bottle."

"Yes, Miss Dill," he said, waving at James to do as she said. "I'm sorry, Miss Dill. It is this footman, you see. He thought the young ladies might—"

"Nonsense," she said sharply, and the butler, tucking his chin against his chest, bowed and backed away.

When James returned, he had an open bottle of champagne and four fresh glasses on the tray. Dillie tasted hers and nodded knowingly.

"Much better," she said, giggling at the girls. "Drink up, ladies."

When the ladies finally retired to the drawing room, Missy sat down at the pianoforte and began playing a mournful tune about lost love. The others soon joined in, their voices slightly off-key, though not one of them noticed.

When the song was over, Angelica said petulantly, "That song's more like a dirge than a love song. Let's play a game."

"Sh! Sh! Come here, girls," said Dillie, motioning the girls closer by waving at them unevenly. "Enough singing. I've a mind to tell you a story or two," she added, patting the sofa where she sat.

"But, Dillie, dear Dillie," began Felicity with a hiccough, "we're too old for bedtime stories."

Dillie shook her head and motioned them even closer. Missy pulled up a chair. Felicity sank down on the stool at Dillie's feet, and Angelica, who had had more champagne than the others, sat down beside the older woman, propping herself up on Dillie's shoulder, humming softly.

"It's not that kind of story," said Dillie, her words

running together slightly, though she felt perfectly sober.

"Then what kind is it?" asked Missy, grinning sleepily; wine always made her sleepy.

"It's a love story," said Dillie, sitting back suddenly. Her unexpected movement caused Angelica to fall forward, almost slipping to the floor, but Felicity pushed her back.

There they all sat, huddled close, their gowns looking like a rainbow: green, purple, pink, and yellow.

"It was long ago, so long ago. Admiral Tupperman was only a first mate then, but he was such a nice young man. I might have set my cap for him, but he had no means to keep me, of course."

"Did you love him very much?" asked the tender-hearted Felicity, her voice catching on a sob.

"No, no, it was nothing like that. Now, Geoffrey, dear Geoffrey, that is another story." She swung her head around, looking at each girl in turn, and said, "We were to be married, but he died in a duel, you know."

"Yes, yes, but what about the admiral?" said Missy.

"It wasn't Tupper, but Anthony, his captain, who caught my eye." Dillie giggled and winked. "Or should I say, I caught him . . . his. We met at an assembly in Bath. Bath was all the crack back then. Everyone went to Bath in the summer." She paused a moment, lost in the past.

Missy patted Dillie's knee to bring her back to the present.

"The story, Dillie. About Anthony," said Missy.

"Yes, about Anthony," said Felicity.

"Oh, yes. Anthony was there on leave. His wife was

gone, so he didn't have anyone to talk to. Then he saw me. I remember I wore lavender that night; my mother wouldn't allow me to wear mourning for Geoffrey any longer, but I couldn't bring myself to wear anything bright and gay."

"What color was your hair, Dillie?" asked Angelica.

"It was brown, dark like Missy's. Dear Anthony always loved to run his hands through it."

"But you never married," said Missy, frowning with concentration.

"We couldn't, not with his wife still alive. He never went back to her, of course, but there was no question of divorce. There was a child, you see."

Felicity gasped, and Dillie said quickly, "Not mine. His wife's. She had run away with another man, leaving the boy with Anthony, so he didn't dare risk a scandal."

"How sad," said Missy. "What happened?"

"What happened? Why, I stayed with Anthony. Then one time—we had been together ten years—he went to sea and never came back. I thought my heart would break."

Felicity began to sob, and Dillie patted the top of her head, tears running down her own face. "There, there, you sweet child. Don't cry. I didn't mean to make you cry."

Angelica threw her arms around Dillie's neck, saying, "Oh, Dillie," over and over.

Disengaging herself, Dillie wiped her face with her sodden handkerchief and blew her nose. "There now. Enough of that nonsense."

She looked at each girl in turn, then said soberly, "I know I am a silly old woman, and I have known you girls such a short time, but it is as if you were all my daughters, the daughters I never had. When we came home last night, I feared Garrett would send me away. I don't think I could bear it," she confessed, sniffling into the handkerchief.

They hugged awkwardly, pledging to keep Dillie with them always so she need never be alone again.

"Now, girls, I really think we should go to bed. We should do as Garrett said and get a good night's sleep."

"Yes, Dillie," chorused the three girls.

Linking arms, Felicity and Missy followed Angelica and Dillie up the stairs to their rooms. When Missy was dressed for bed, she knocked on the connecting door to Felicity's room.

"Come in, Missy," called Felicity.

"You are not asleep yet?" asked Missy, crossing the room and sitting on the side of her sister's bed.

"No, I don't think I can sleep."

"What is wrong, dear?"

"The story Dillie told us—it is so sad."

"I know. We must do all we can to make certain Garrett does not turn Dillie off."

"But what will happen to her when the Season is over?" asked Felicity, her eyes filling with tears again. "Have you thought of that?"

"Now, now, we will think of something. Perhaps we can ask the admiral to help."

Felicity sat up, her face shining with excitement. "Wouldn't it be wonderful if he married her!"

"Wonderful, but I don't think we can ask him to do that," said Missy.

"Not ask him, but perhaps show him the way. Let

me think on it," said the younger girl, lying back against the soft pillow, her expression pensive.

"When you have a plan, Felicity, and I know you will, just let me know if I can be of help. Good night, dear," said Missy, rising and returning to her own room.

She climbed into the bed and pulled the covers up under her chin. Thanks to the combination of two glasses of champagne and a convivial evening, Missy slept without dreams disturbing her rest. Not once did she dream of Garrett.

Could she help it if he was the first thing on her mind in the morning?

Seven

Garrett, for all his experience with women, had very little knowledge about them. When he received the letter from Missy's steward asking his advice on several matters relating to the farm and its tenants, he jumped at the excuse for his first visit to his own estate, the famed Lambert Racing Stables.

He worried, however, how Dillie would view his desertion for a week in the middle of the Season. He announced his intentions at dinner that night, but Dillie, preparing to leave for a musicale and a rout with her charges, appeared delighted with the prospect of his departure.

Slightly miffed, Garrett asked, "Missy, is there anything I can do for you while I am there? Any commission you need me to perform? What about you, Felicity?"

"No, thank you, Garrett. I can think of nothing," said Felicity.

Missy, on the other hand, asked the impossible. "If you don't mind terribly, Garrett, I should like to go with you."

"I'm afraid that's not possible," he replied, smiling affably.

"Why not? It is my home, after all."

"Of course, and always will be, if you wish, but this is just business," said Garrett. "You would be bored, and I know you have countless diversions to keep you in London."

"Garrett, I am never bored by any business that concerns Lambert Farm," she said quietly.

"But you have accepted the invitations here; you have balls to attend and gentlemen to charm," he persisted despite reading rebellion in her beautiful, stormy eyes.

"I don't think you understand, Garrett. You need me. No one else can explain."

"I know you want to believe that, Missy, but your steward can explain anything that needs to be explained. And let me assure you, I am not completely ignorant about the workings of an estate. I did grow up helping my own father and brother, and our family seat alone is twice the size of Lambert Farm."

Missy swallowed hard and bit her bottom lip; her eyes glinted with unexpressed anger, but she kept her tongue. How many times had her father arrogantly dismissed her from his study when she had tried to point out some flaw in his planning? And how many times had he later sought her out and asked her to help him work out some insurmountable problem? And she had. She always did.

As for Price, he was a dear friend and an excellent steward, but he knew absolutely nothing about the breeding farm. At least he realized it and had never attempted to interfere, leaving that aspect of the estate to her since her father's illness and demise.

And Garrett? He was deluding himself if he

thought his training as a gentleman farmer qualified him to take up the reins at the stables. Running the estate, the farm, being a landlord: those were things he could manage. But he had never run a breeding farm whose sole purpose was to breed for speed, to breed for the next derby winner.

He would be wishing she had come along; she knew it as certainly as she knew the sun would rise in the morning.

And she wouldn't let him down.

Still seething, Missy pulled her chair slightly apart from where Garrett and the others were seated, listening politely to Lady Philpot's spotted daughter warble out an aria, occasionally hitting the correct note. When it was over, they applauded politely at first, then more enthusiastically as the girl stepped off the raised platform that served as a stage.

"Next we have another treat for you, ladies and gentlemen," said their hostess, a purple-turbaned matron whose figure was twice as slender as her daughter's and who didn't mind showing off her best attributes in a gown with a scandalously low neckline.

"Not the other daughter," whispered the gentleman to Missy's left.

She flashed him a smile, and then it broadened when she recognized Fitzsimmons Worth.

"Good evening, sir," she said, moving her skirts to one side so he could settle into his chair more comfortably.

"Good evening to you, my dear Miss Lambert. Or should I say Lady Miss?" he asked, winking at her.

"How in the world . . . ?"

"I have my sources, Miss Lambert," he said, laying his finger along the side of his nose.

Missy shrugged and turned back toward the stage, where the next performer was sitting down at a large harp.

"The other daughter?" whispered Missy.

"No, someone else's, but I believe she is supposed to be quite good. We shall see," said Mr. Worth.

The harpist was very talented, and the audience stayed willingly in their seats until the performance was over.

"I have always wanted to learn how to play the harp," confessed Missy to Mr. Worth.

"As the saying goes, my dear, it is never too late," he responded.

"For what?" asked Garrett, leaning forward to glare at his old rival.

Missy lifted her chin and answered, "To learn to play the harp, if you must know, Cousin Garrett."

"Oh," he said, turning back to answer some comment from Dillie, but Missy had the feeling he was listening to her conversation all the same.

"I vow I am parched, Mr. Worth. Might we go in search of some refreshments?"

Shooting Garrett a triumphant smirk, Worth offered his arm and said quickly, "Certainly, dear lady. I daresay there is some champagne to be had. Lady Philpot is always a most generous hostess." He leaned close to her ear and added outrageously, "That is why everyone still attends her musicales despite her daughters' performances."

"You are being wicked, Mr. Worth. I dare not leave

your company for fear of what you will say of me in
my absence," said Missy, wondering where the coquette had been hiding in her all these years. There
was just something about this man with his sandy-
colored hair and boyish charm that brought out the
flirt in her.

"Ah, you encourage me to be outrageous then, my
dear lady, if it keeps you by my side," came his suave
rejoinder.

Missy trilled a laugh, sounding as practiced as Angelica's best. Chuckling under her breath at herself,
she accepted the glass of champagne Mr. Worth offered, her eyes sparkling like the golden liquid.

"Missy, they are about to begin again," said Garrett,
stepping between his ward and his rival.

"Then by all means, Garrett, return to the audience. I find I am enjoying my conversation with Mr.
Worth too much to interrupt it right now. I feel certain I can count on him to escort me back later."

"Missy," growled Garrett, but he knew there was
nothing he could do, short of causing a scene. And
for all the world knew, and Missy, too, Fitz Worth was
all a gentleman should be. "Very well," he said, stalking away.

Missy managed not to sigh, but the merriment had
definitely fled from the evening for her. Still, he
ought to know why she was so upset with him, and
yet it appeared he had no idea. Men!

"Things going badly with the dictatorial guardian?" asked her companion, his boyish smile inviting
her to confide in him.

Missy resisted the temptation to speak ill of Garrett;

after all, he couldn't help it if her feelings for him were all tied up in knots.

Instead, she smiled at Mr. Worth and confided, "No, no; it is just that he is going to visit Lambert Farm tomorrow, and he doesn't wish to take me."

"The beast!" exclaimed Mr. Worth, hand over heart. His eyes twinkling, he added softly, "Of course, I cannot be too indignant on your behalf, Miss Lambert, if he refuses to take you away from London right now."

"Oh, it is not that. I just want to go home, if only for a few days. I miss it so."

"It is a beautiful part of the country," he said.

"Yes, and then there is the matter of my horse. I did so hate to leave in the midst of his training."

"Your horse? A new prospect? Someone a betting man should know about?" he asked with exaggerated eagerness, causing her to giggle.

"I don't even know if he will be ready to race this year. He's a little high-strung. I am trying to calm him down; allow him to get used to being around noise and such."

"I should think that would be a difficult task in the middle of Yorkshire. Why don't you bring him to London?"

"Oh, I don't know," she said, though the idea began to take hold.

"But I guess he is not really yours to do with as you please, is he? He must belong to Wyndridge now."

"No, no, King's Shilling is mine, not Lambert Farm's. He's my hope for the future. If he is as successful at the track as I know he will be, I could start my own stable," said Missy.

"Then why not bring him to London? Surely Wyndridge would be willing to stand the nonsense of stabling the beast. Especially for you," he added.

"I suppose, but I would have to look after him myself, or else bring along my stable manager. It could become quite complicated." Frowning, Missy sighed.

"It is a shame, however. I know I could arrange a match race for him. You wouldn't even have to wait for Newmarket."

"Really?"

"Really. Only say the word," promised Worth with his best disarming smile.

"I will think about it. First, however, I will have to convince Garrett to allow me to accompany him to Yorkshire. It won't be easy," she said, grimacing at the thought of the altercation.

"A room and accommodations for my people and horses, landlord," said Garrett, climbing down from the carriage and stretching mightily.

"Of course, sir. Right this way. Your people can drive around to the stables in the rear. They will be well taken care of, as you will be, too," said the round man, rubbing his hands together gleefully. It was a small inn, but well kept, bespeaking its quality and prosperity.

"Seth, see to the animals first. Then yourself," said Garrett, shaking his finger at the young groom who was known for eating more than everyone else in the stables combined.

"Lud, Sir Garrett, ye know I takes care of th' cattle first," he replied, looking hurt.

"Just see that you do," said Garrett.

In the boot of the carriage, Missy was feeling exceedingly cramped, bruised, and sore. She shifted her weight, turning toward the leather covering, trying to lift it and peek outside. It was stiff and wouldn't budge. She felt panic rising; since Garrett hadn't planned to stay away long, he had stowed his small case under the seat instead of in the boot. What if they never opened it? What if—

"Help! Help!" she cried. When there was no response, her voice rose, and she yelped pitifully, "Please let me out!"

She heard someone pulling at the covering, and suddenly soft light flooded her tiny compartment.

"Bloody 'ell," said Seth, reaching in and helping her alight.

"Thank you, Seth. Thank you so much," she whispered, taking in her surroundings quickly.

"Beggin' yer pardon, miss, but what th' . . . that is, what were you doin' in th' boot?"

"I . . . I was playing a joke on Sir Garrett," she lied. Well, she thought, *perhaps it didn't count as a true lie.* She was playing something . . . a trick.

Something you swore you never did, said a persistent voice in her head. Missy smiled at the groom winningly.

"What you goin' t' do now, miss?" he asked, looking her up and down.

Missy blushed from the top of her smock to the bottom of her boots. Nervously, she picked at a thread on her breeches, unable to meet the groom's eye.

"I suppose I should go and speak to Sir Garrett," she said.

"Speak to . . . in those clothes . . . in the public house?"

"Well, then perhaps we can sneak into his room," Missy supplied helpfully.

"Sneak into . . . I'd as lief play with fire, miss."

"Then perhaps you can point me in the right direction, Seth. I am very tired and very hungry, and I am losing patience," she said, her voice rising slightly as she became the haughty lady of the manor.

Hesitating only a second more, the unfortunate groom handed her the small case she had packed and led the way to the back of the inn.

"See that? It leads to the kitchens. Just put yer head down and mumble somethin' about taking this to yer master. They'll show you th' way."

Missy grinned at him and turned toward the house.

"Good luck," he added gruffly before hurrying back the way they had come. "She'll need it."

Missy marveled at the ease with which she gained access to Garrett's empty room. She sighed, a mixture of relief and disappointment, to discover he was downstairs. Placing her case near the door, she sat down on the bed to wait. Her stomach growled, but she forced herself to ignore it.

Weariness overcame her, and she lay back, falling sound asleep.

* * *

Garrett yawned and blinked twice before he found the strength to turn the latch on his door. He couldn't remember ever feeling so pulled. He shut the door, his toe striking an object just inside the threshold. Frowning, he held his candle down and discovered an unfamiliar case.

"Humph," he murmured, picking it up and setting it out in the corridor before closing the door again. A servant must have mistaken it for his; no doubt someone would be looking for it in the morning.

His back to the bed, Garrett shrugged out of his coat and waistcoat. After untying his cravat, he removed his shirt. He sat down and began tugging at his boot heel, suddenly wishing he had allowed the finicky Anderson to accompany him. But he hadn't wanted to arrive like a grand dame, traveling with her entourage of servants and luggage.

There! The boot gave way, and he caught himself with one elbow before falling backwards.

"Mmmm."

Garrett leapt to his feet, spinning around, his eyes wide.

"What the deuce!" he exclaimed, grabbing the candle from the bedside table and holding it high above the bed.

"Devil take me," he ground out, scowling at the sleeping figure of his eldest, and without a doubt, most stubborn ward. How in the world had she stayed hidden away? The boot, of course, but what a dreadful way to travel. So much the better!

He reached out to shake her, to throttle her, but she sighed and tucked her hand under her cheek, arresting Garrett's intention and, to some extent, his ire.

He sought out the only chair in the small room and removed his other boot, his mind working feverishly.

No one knew she was here. Well, he felt certain her sister knew, but not for the world would she reveal such a juicy tidbit of gossip about Missy.

Seth might know, and if he had known since London, Garrett vowed to sack him and then shoot him.

Garrett's thoughts were interrupted by a mighty yawn. He stared at the sleeping figure in the bed, drawn up into a ball. Probably cold, he thought with a grunt of satisfaction.

She was in that silly garb again. He looked around and spied the large-brimmed straw hat. She still wore her boots. He wondered if he should attempt to remove them, but the thought brought forth all sorts of comfortable, intimate images, and he decided that since she had been sleeping well so far, he shouldn't take the chance of disturbing her.

He shivered and spent a few minutes adding another log on the pitiful fire before another shiver overtook him.

"Demmed if I'll catch my death because of you," he said quietly and crossed the room to the bed, sitting down on the edge gingerly.

Missy had fallen asleep on top of the counterpane, so he threw this over her, tucking it around her, trying to remember that she was his ward, his responsibility, and not the soft, round female he knew her to be.

Then he slipped between the sheets, turned his

back to Missy, and promised himself he would hug the edge of the bed until morning—even if he got precious little sleep.

Missy thought she was drowning, the feeling so powerful that it pulled her out of her nightmare sharply. She blinked and realized the blanket had somehow covered her face, and she could hardly breathe. Her arms felt pinioned to her sides, and she struggled to free them and tear the blanket away.

Success! she thought, gulping down a great breath of air and opening her mouth to scream.

Garrett clamped his hand over her mouth, his deep green eyes daring her to make a sound. Panicking, only half awake, Missy turned her head and bit his fingers.

"Devil seize you, girl!" he yelled, pushing away violently, nursing his hand and falling to the floor with a loud thump.

Missy stood up in the bed, swaying like a drunken sailor, trying to keep her legs from buckling beneath her.

"Devil seize *you!*" she cried, glaring at him.

"Now, Missy," began Garrett, pushing up on the side of the bed and climbing to his feet.

His movement pressed the mattress down, and Missy pitched headlong into his chest, knocking him off his feet again. She landed on top of him with another thud.

She scrambled off of him, legs flailing, hands pushing, and booted foot connecting, catching Garrett in exactly the wrong spot.

A loud knocking on the door was followed by an angry, "What's going on in there?"

Gasping for air, Garrett could say nothing.

Wide-eyed, Missy looked at Garrett. She sat up and lowered her voice, saying gruffly, "Nothing. Had a nightmare. Fell out of bed."

They waited breathlessly while the speaker considered his options and said crossly, "Just be quiet. Some people are trying to sleep."

"Sorry," said Missy manfully, as their visitor's footsteps trailed away.

Missy's blue eyes, now wide open, met the now recovered Garrett's. His eyes began to twinkle, the corners crinkled, and his chest began to shake with silent laughter.

Missy giggled.

"Sh!" he said, sitting up and facing her. "We don't want our friend coming back," he whispered.

Missy shook her head, biting her lip. But she looked back in those smiling eyes and began to giggle uncontrollably. Her laughter was contagious, and Garrett was soon laughing out loud, his shoulders shaking, wiping tears from his eyes.

The knocking recommenced.

"Now you've done it," whispered Missy.

Garrett put a finger to his lips and went to the door, opening it an inch or two and peering outside.

"I'm sorry to disturb you, Sir Garrett," said the landlord, still dressed in his sleeping attire and wearing his nightcap. In the background lurked two other guests.

"Think nothing of it, my good man," Garrett said, giving the man his winning smile.

The landlord grimaced, glancing over his shoulder at the others. "I try to run a quiet establishment, and these are regular customers," he explained apologetically.

"I understand. I'll keep it down."

"If that's one of my maids you have in—"

"Not at all. Why would you think that? Oh, the laughter. Yes, yes, but I find laughter is the best way to wake up in the morning. I try to think of funny things and make myself laugh; it always starts my day out so nicely. But I do apologize; sometimes I get a little carried away," he said, chuckling self-deprecatingly.

"I'll try to keep it quieter," he added, his voice louder for the benefit of the other guests.

"Thank you, Sir Garrett," said the landlord, backing away.

Garrett closed the door. He remained where he was, facing it, wondering if it was safe to turn around. If Missy started laughing again. . . .

But Missy had sobered completely. The realization of what had happened had hit her forcefully. Any other time, she would have gone into the whoops over Garrett's implausible explanation, but the gravity of their situation extinguished her amusement.

Garrett turned to face her, his own expression sober.

"What now, Missy?" he asked quietly, his voice barely above a whisper.

"What do you mean?" she breathed.

"We have spent the night together in an inn. You have been compromised. I have been dishonorable to you, one of my wards. Do we find the nearest church?" he asked with brutal honesty.

The secret part of Missy screamed, *Yes!* Out loud, she said sensibly, "I don't see why we should. No one who knows us will ever find out. Even the landlord only suspects you have a female in the room. And while it might be a trifle unusual for me to accompany you, with only a groom, on such a journey, no one in the house back in London will quibble about it. In Yorkshire, they won't think anything of it. How else was I to get home, if not with you?"

Garrett expelled a pent-up breath. *Of relief,* thought Missy sourly.

"Very well. We won't tell anyone your accompanying me was not planned. You will remain in your countryman garb until we leave the inn. Somewhere along the road, you can change into your gown. I assume you have a gown."

Missy looked at the door, frowning. "I did have one, in my case. Where is it?"

Garrett muttered something under his breath, jerked the door open, and retrieved the leather case.

"That's all I need, for the landlord to find a bandbox outside my door containing a lady's gown."

Missy stifled a giggle and accepted the case. Her stomach let out a loud growl.

"Excuse me," she whispered, color flooding her face.

"When did you last eat?" he demanded.

"Yesterday morning."

"Sit down. I will go downstairs and get a tray."

"But won't they wonder?"

"Let them. I am too famished to care," he replied, winking at her before leaving the room.

Missy waited anxiously for his return. She kept replaying her awakening in her mind. Where exactly had Garrett been? Surely he hadn't been in bed with her! Not that she suspected him of any impropriety, of course. He was too much the gentleman for that. "Unfortunately," she muttered to herself, then shook her head at such a scandalous thought.

Taking down her plaited hair, she crossed to the dressing table and made use of Garrett's comb, staring at herself all the while, occasionally shaking her head.

"All you had to do was say yes," she told her image.

She spun around to find Garrett closing the door behind him. Her eyes flew to his face. Had he heard her? But no, he wasn't even looking her way.

"I think there's enough here for the both of us. But if you're still hungry after we leave, we can stop and eat again this morning," he said, setting the heavy tray on the bedside table and pulling the chair up to it.

Garrett settled on the edge of the bed and watched her fill her plate, his expression inscrutable. Finally, he helped himself.

"This is beautiful country, Missy. I can understand why you love it so," said Garrett as they crossed the Swale River.

Stopping the carriage, he allowed his team to drink from the cool, clear water while he gazed across the pebble-strewn bank to the green fields beyond.

"I have always loved it. Though I enjoyed going to Newmarket and Ascot, I was always happy to be back home," said Missy, a dreamy smile curving her lips. "We'll be there soon."

They rode in companionable silence for another hour. When they rounded the last bend in the road, Missy sat forward, straining to see the gateway to home. With a sigh, and a contented smile for Garrett, she sat back against the leather seat, studying his face as they bowled up the long drive.

On the left was a low stone wall, beyond which the green pasture was dotted with sheep. To the right the pasture was lined by a rail fence, built high and sturdy.

The carriage slowed as they came abreast of a group of mares and foals grazing in the late afternoon sun.

"What do you think?" Missy asked, her tone like a child's who has done his best and hopes his parents approve.

Garrett pulled back on the ribbons, bringing his team to a stop. He turned his gaze from the scene of pastoral harmony and settled it on his ward. The smile on his lips and the warmth in his shining eyes was all the answer Missy needed.

"I knew you would love it, too," she whispered.

"You will think me foolish, I know, but I feel as if I have come home," he replied.

"Not foolish, Garrett. Not at all," she said, slipping her hand through the crook of his arm as they continued up the drive.

"Lady Miss, how good it is to see you," said McMann, toddling down the steps of the house.

"It's so good to be home," she said, hopping to the ground without waiting for assistance and throwing her arms around the old man's neck. He held her away from him, beaming like a besotted grandfather.

"Now then, child, didn't we teach you any better than that?" he asked, blushing with pleasure.

"Of course, but you know how wayward I can be," she teased. "Garrett, this is McMann, our butler and my friend. And Price! How wonderful to see you!" she exclaimed, running toward a young man with sandy hair and practically knocking him off his feet with a great bear hug.

Dragging him forward, she chattered in a manner so shocking that Garrett kept wondering where the real Missy Lambert had gotten to.

"Price, this is Sir Garrett Wyndridge. Garrett, this is Price Matthews, my steward. That is, the estate steward," she amended, brought up short by the awkward realization that she could no longer call them her butler or her bailiff. Blushing with confusion, she stood aside silently as the two men sized each other up, shaking hands and exchanging pleasantries.

"If you don't mind, I'd like to look over the books immediately, Mr. Matthews."

"Certainly. I brought everything to Missy's study in anticipation of your request," said Price before turning to his childhood friend and teasing, "I had no idea you would be coming, Missy. I thought you'd be too caught up in the social whirl to take time for a visit."

Missy gave him a withering look and swept past him into the house, pausing a moment to inhale deeply the fragrance of home. She couldn't identify the source, but there was a distinctive scent. Occasionally she would find a hint of it elsewhere; it was like being transported back to the front hall at home.

"Where should I put Sir Garrett, Lady Miss? I had Sally air the master's old room, but that's just across the hall from your room. I didn't know you would be coming, you see. Should I put him in the other wing?" asked the butler anxiously.

"I see no reason to change anything, McMann. Sir Garrett is the master, and he should have Papa's old room. We will be fine. Will you show him to his room? I want to change and go out to the stables."

"Of course, miss. You run along," said the old man, shaking his head, but he smiled at her fondly as she disappeared up the stairs.

The two men spent an hour pouring over Matthews's carefully kept ledgers. At the end of this time, Garrett pushed away from the desk, well pleased with his bailiff. He rose and poured two large measures of brandy, offering one to Matthews before resuming his seat behind the battered desk.

"I think that's enough, Mr. Matthews. If the army kept such excellent records, everything would move much more efficiently."

Across from his new employer, Price's jaw dropped. After enduring Garrett's probing interrogation, he had expected a mild reprimand at the very least. His anger and defensiveness had grown with each question, and Garrett's praise effectively took the wind out of his sails.

"Why, thank you, sir," Price managed to say.

"Tell me about yourself, Matthews. You seem to be more one of the family than a mere bailiff."

"My father and Rupert Lambert were at school together, practically inseparable. My father was the youngest of five sons. My uncle is Sir Hubert Matthews; perhaps you have heard of him."

Garrett grunted and nodded, taking another sip of the brandy.

"My father loved farming, so Uncle Rupert—Lord Lambert, that is—hired him to run the farm while Uncle Rupert concentrated on the horseracing and breeding. He was very generous, even deeding over a house and a small plot of land to my father. This has been my home all my life. When Lord Lambert died, he left me more land."

"I see. And Missy?"

The two men locked gazes, each interpreting the other man's intentions. Price looked away first.

"I make no excuses, Sir Garrett. I suppose I would have married Missy long ago if she would have had me. But she considers me a brother. Besides, when it's a choice between a husband and her horses, she'll choose her horses every time."

"I see." Garrett rose, extending his hand and saying, "Thank you, Mr. Matthews. I hope you intend to continue managing the farm for me. I do want to reside here most of the year, but until other matters are settled with my wards, I'm afraid I must remain in London."

"Of course, and I am happy to remain. May I be frank, Sir Garrett?" Garrett nodded, and Price continued, "I have been very concerned about Missy and

Felicity since they left. Having met you, however, I feel much more at ease."

"Thank you, Mr. Matthews. I will endeavor to earn that confidence."

All the greetings had been exchanged, and the training paddock cleared. King's Shilling whickered softly when Missy opened his stall and entered, crooning softly. He took the bite of apple she offered and then butted his big head against her chest while she stroked his glossy neck.

"Let's see what you remember, big boy. Has Roberts been able to keep you fit while I was gone?" Missy braced herself as he pushed against her again, nuzzling her hand to see if she had brought another treat. Missy worked the bit into his mouth and expertly slipped the head strap over his ears.

She led him down the silent row of stalls and into the paddock. The sunbeams filtering through the nearby trees bathed the earth in golden light. It was dusk, but she couldn't have waited until morning to see the powerful stallion again, to feel the earth tremble as he cantered around her, his ears pricked forward, listening to her every command. To Missy, King's movements were like poetry, his gait as smooth as glass.

"So, my beauty, you haven't forgotten," she murmured as she let the rope lengthen. "Who knows, we may get you to Ascot this year yet," she added hopefully.

"Lad," called Garrett from the paddock fence.

Missy grinned to herself and refused to turn

around, reaching up with one hand to tug her cap down more firmly.

"Lad!" he called, more loudly this time. "Excuse me, but where is everyone?" he said, hopping easily over the fence when the boy still didn't acknowledge him.

"Boy!" he roared in his best military voice, startling the horse and Missy.

She spun around just as King's Shilling broke stride, galloping wildly, veering away from Garrett and heading straight for his mistress, picking up speed as he closed the gap quickly. Missy tried to pull in the long lead rope, but she wasn't fast enough.

Too late did Garrett recognize Missy. When he did, he rushed forward, leaping through the air and knocking her to the ground. The rope was jerked out of her hands as the stallion flew past them and sailed over the fence, the long lead trailing dangerously in his wake.

Pushing Garrett off, Missy snapped, "Of all the ad-dle-pated, want-witted things to do! What the devil were you trying to do?"

"How about saving your bloody life," he returned.

"I didn't need to be saved until you came out here shouting loud enough to wake the dead!"

"If you had answered—Where are you going?" he demanded, following on her heels as she ran toward the stables.

"I have to go after him," she said.

"It's almost dark!" exclaimed Garrett.

Missy stopped in her tracks, almost causing Garrett to collide with her.

"That is why I have to go after him, Garrett," she

said, as if explaining a problem to a child. "Assuming he doesn't get tangled in his rope, King's Shilling will be in the next county by morning."

"Then we'll send the grooms," said Garrett.

"You just don't understand," she said, entering one of the stalls and leading out a bay mare. "King's Shilling won't let anyone but me handle him. Me and Roberts. I can't send the grooms." She bridled the mare and swung onto her back.

"Don't worry. I see very well in the dark."

When she was gone, Garrett roared, "Roberts!"

Weary but triumphant, Missy rode into the stables by the light of the moon. Roberts, the head groom, and Garrett followed alongside. For once, King's Shilling didn't shy away from them; he was too weary, too.

Missy rubbed him down before returning to the house. Garrett had gone ahead, ordering a hot bath for both himself and Missy. He drank a bottle of Cook's ale and ate a huge sandwich before sinking into the steamy water.

By the time Missy climbed the stairs to her room, Garrett was feeling much more the thing. He had left his door open so he could speak to her when she arrived.

"Missy, I am sorry," said Garrett.

She paused, her hand on the latch, the ghost of a polite smile on her exhausted face. "I know, Garrett. And I apologize for all those terrible things I said . . . or thought," she added, chuckling. "I was amused that you didn't recognize me. I should have answered you instead of playing a foolish trick on you. It was as much my fault as it was yours."

Garret stepped closer, putting his hand on her shoulder. He could feel her tremble at his touch. "You're quite a woman, Missy Lambert. Most ladies would not be as candid."

"I just didn't want you to feel bad when it wasn't your fault. Good night, Garrett," she added, turning away.

"Good night."

Eight

Garrett had fallen in love with his new home at first sight, from the woolly sheep to the newest foal. The people, too, were anxious to please and went out of their way to make him feel welcome. He had expected to have to win their approval and respect, but they offered it freely.

It never occurred to him that Missy, or Lady Miss as the servants and stable help called her, had purposely smoothed the way for him. Assembling the household servants, she had praised Garrett for his generosity to her and her sister, an attribute they heartily applauded. At the stables, when they had finally settled King's Shilling into his stall for the night, Missy had told Roberts and his grooms about Garrett's well-run mews in London, about his even-handedness with all his people.

So from Cook to the potboy, from Roberts to the boy mucking out the stalls, everyone was happy to greet the new master of Lambert Farm and welcome him with open arms.

"Roberts," said Garrett, looking in on King's Shilling early the next morning, "tell me why your mistress sets such store by this stallion."

"That's easy enough, Sir Garrett. King's dam was her favorite mare. The old baron, just before he died, accepted a challenge for a match race. It was a foolish race to begin with. Lady Miss kept telling him he couldn't hope to win, and she's almost always right. Anyway, the wager was for the mare, and she was in foal with King's Shilling at the time. It fair broke her heart to give the mare up. I heard tell she died after foaling."

"So Lady Miss bought her colt and brought him back here," commented Garrett, beginning to understand.

"Aye, but not until he was almost two years old; wild as a banshee he was. He had great welts across his back where the bastard had beaten him," said the head groom, turning his head and spitting to show his disapproval of such cruelty.

"Does she ride him?"

"Yes; she can ride him, and so can I, but no one else dares. And the worst is the way he reacts every time he's startled or sees a riding crop or whip. He bolts every time, completely out of control."

"Sounds to me like he would be better off if he were put down," said Garrett. "At his age—I judge he's about five or six—he's not likely to change."

"Perhaps, but he has come such a long way. And th' mistress, she would never have him destroyed."

The memory of the terror he had felt when he had seen the stallion galloping straight for Missy still fresh in his mind, Garrett faced the head groom and said, "But she's not the mistress here anymore."

Garrett detected a flash of mutiny in the head groom's eyes. Then Roberts shook his head, favoring his new master with a pitying look. "I suppose you don't know that King's Shilling belongs to Miss Lambert personally. Lambert Racing didn't buy him; she did." With this, the groom walked away.

Deep in thought, Garrett wandered back toward the house and found Missy in the breakfast room picking at the remains of her food and sipping cold coffee.

"Good morning, Missy," he said cheerily, all the while wondering how he would persuade her to get rid of her dangerous pet.

"Good morning, Garrett," she replied, stealing sidelong glances at him, but refusing to meet his eyes. "Have you been out riding?"

"No, I just went for a stroll. It's such a lovely morning. I quite understand your reluctance to exchange this idyllic setting for the soot and grime of London. Especially in early March when my first, uh, invitation arrived."

She looked up then and demanded suspiciously, "Are you roasting me, Garrett?"

"Perhaps just a little, Missy. But I do appreciate the beauty of the place. How old is the house?"

"It was built by my great-grandfather, the first Baron Lambert, back in 1750 after the original manor house burned. It is not as grand as some country homes, of course, but we have always been comfortable here. Some of the barns date back to 1600, but they have been well maintained. And the new one for the broodmares is beyond the rise out there; Papa had drawn up the plans when he became ill," she said, pointing toward the window which faced the back of the house.

"Very impressive. And the breeding program is based on the stud, old King Herod?" Not, Garrett admitted privately, the usual topic of conversation over breakfast with a lady, but nothing about Missy was in the usual way.

"We also have Herod's Folly, who was quite successful on the track. He's ten years old. I, uh, I had hoped to introduce another stud, but I suppose that will be up to you now."

"Yes, but I'll need some help sorting all this out. Who would be the best man to consult, Matthews or Roberts?"

Missy frowned and said proudly, "But I am the one you need to consult, Garrett. I tried to tell you that in London, but you wouldn't listen. Anything you want to know about Lambert Farm, you need only ask me."

"For some things like family history, but I'm talking about learning the business of racehorse husbandry and of managing the day-to-day stable management. I feel Lambert Farms will only continue successfully if the master knows at least as much as his best men."

Missy shoved back from the table, her chair crashing to the floor behind her. "Of all the arrogant . . . I should have known you were no different from Papa! You're all the same!"

Garrett jumped up, preparing to follow, but his way was suddenly blocked by McMann, toddling into the room with a fresh pot of coffee.

"Cook wants to know what else you might like, Sir

Garrett. She has some kidney pie, and of course can always cook up several rashers of bacon and some eggs. Anything you like; you need only ask," said the smiling old man, pouring a cup of coffee for his new employer.

Garrett took a deep breath and settled back into his chair. "I am famished, McMann. Tell Cook to send in the pie immediately and follow it with the bacon and eggs."

The butler nodded and headed for the door. Garrett stopped him with, "And, McMann, please send word to Roberts that I wish to see him in the study in an hour."

"Very good, sir."

"Hello, Roberts. Have a seat," said Garrett, looking up from the same ledger page he had been studying for the past fifteen minutes.

The head groom obeyed and remained silent until Garrett looked up, his brow creased by a frown.

"I'm going to need your help deciphering these, I'm afraid," said Garrett, pushing the book toward Roberts, who looked at the page obligingly while a frown grew on his own weathered brow.

"I know everyone has their own system of book-keeping, but you'll have to help me with this, Roberts."

After another moment, Roberts sat back, shaking his head. "I'm sorry, sir, I can't help with this. I never kept the books. Lady Miss—Miss Lambert, that is— hired me because I knew about horses and breeding.

I'm not much of a dab hand with the pen, I'm afraid."

"I see. How long have you worked for the Lambert family?"

"Six years, sir."

"Then you knew the old baron?"

"Of course. He was beginning to slow down a bit when I arrived. He was showing signs of his illness even then. It was, as I said, Miss Lambert who hired me."

"But you don't keep the books on the stables," said Garrett again.

"No, sir."

"Very well. That will be all then," said Garrett pensively.

Roberts paused at the door and asked, "Will you be wanting that tour of the estate this morning, sir?"

"What? No, no. I think I will just go for a ride on my own. Would you select a mount for me? I'll be down in thirty minutes or so."

"Certainly, sir. My pleasure."

Garrett left the study and the ledgers after a few more minutes of frustrated attempts to decode the entries. He wandered through the downstairs rooms without finding a soul. He was coming to realize that the house was very sparsely manned while the stables were absolutely teeming with grooms.

Though he'd hoped to discover Missy and smooth her ruffled feathers, his luck was out. She was probably miles from home, mounted on that maniac horse of hers, her thoughts on anything and anyone but him.

Not that he cared. . . .

* * *

Missy was indeed astride King's Shilling, sailing over fences, luxuriating in the freedom she had missed so sorely while confined by the streets and mores of London. She wore her comfortable, scandalous breeches, her shirttail tucked into them, her feet shoved into old, scuffed boots. Her long, dark hair streamed down her back, the mass of tangled curls reveling in the absence of pins and sugar water.

She finally reined in at a secluded pool where she and Price had spent happy summer days wading in the cool water and trying to catch elusive fish. Missy slipped King's bridle from his head, replacing it with a rope halter. She untied the lead rope from her waist and secured him to a nearby bush before she sat down and began removing her boots and stockings.

Missy rolled up her trouser legs and stepped into the water, shuffling her feet and stirring up mud as she walked along the edge of the small pond. One side of the pool was open and overlooked the pasture beyond, and she was captured by the beauty of the vista.

Her breath caught in her throat, and she felt hot tears spring to her eyes. Frowning and sniffling, she grinned at King, who gazed at her, his large brown eyes impassive.

Through her tears, Missy giggled, and sloshed her way out of the pool. "Easy," she whispered, approaching King quietly before putting her arms around his neck and burying her head in his mane.

"If only things could stay like they are right now. If only I didn't have to go back to London."

She gave him a final, fierce hug and dropped her arms, her shoulders sagging. Reluctantly, she retrieved her stockings and shoes and began dressing, all the while keeping up a one-sided conversation with her grazing horse.

"You know, things would have been different if Garrett had only fallen head over heels in love with me. Then we could have married, and I would have been able to continue on as before. Not, of course, that that is what I truly wish for—marrying him, that is. I mean, it would only be a way to keep you and Lambert Farms. It's not as if marrying him is my life-long dream. Nor even a recent one. Well, at least, not every night," she admitted candidly to her unresponsive listener.

She looped the lead around King's neck while she removed the halter and put on his bridle. Then, securing the halter and lead, she led the big horse over to a boulder to mount.

Missy's thoughts were troubled as she stopped by two of the tenant farms before finding her way to Price's back door late in the afternoon. She was greeted by his mother, an elderly woman who welcomed Missy warmly.

"He's not in now, Missy, and I don't know when he may be home. You're welcome to come in and have a cup of tea. It's been a long time since we had a nice chat."

"I'd love to, Aunt Sylvia, but I should be getting home. They will be sending out the search parties before long."

"Well, do come back before you leave, my dear. I so want to hear about London."

"I will try," promised Missy, leading King's Shilling back toward the barn where there was a mounting block.

"I see you had the same idea I did," said Garrett, startling Missy, although King took this new presence in stride.

"Must you sneak up on a person?" she snapped.

"I made no effort to sneak up on anyone," he replied. "Just tell me if we are to come to cuffs again, and I promise I will ride away and leave you to yourself. I did hope, however, to speak to Mr. Matthews."

"He's not here, and his mother doesn't know when he'll be back," said Missy. Reluctantly, she added, "I'm sorry, Garrett, I didn't mean to be cross."

"Then heaven help us all when you do mean to be cross," said Garrett, the twinkle in his green eyes robbing his words of offense. Just in case, however, he put up one hand and added hastily, "Friends again?"

"Perhaps," she said solemnly. "At any rate, I shall try to keep my temper with you. I know you don't mean to upset me."

Puzzled, but unwilling to disturb the delicate balance of peace, Garrett nodded and asked, "If you're going home, might I ride with you? I came by way of the road, and I'm sure there's a shorter path home."

"Oh, you went several miles out of the way if you got here by road," she said, allowing Garrett to help her mount. Though she held her breath at his touch, she managed to continue conversing airily as she gradually exhaled. "There is a path worn between the two estates, our families visited so often. Price spent more time at the farm than at home."

"Even today?" asked Garrett, thinking privately that he had been correct in assuming he should question Matthews about the ledgers.

"I suppose he does, though we no longer share lessons together," she said with a chuckle. "He hated coming over for that; he thought he was too good to study with a governess."

"Most boys prefer a male tutor before they are old enough for school," commented Garrett.

"Yes, but his family couldn't afford it, so his father made him submit to Miss Hatchet's rules."

"Hatchet?" queried Garrett, following Missy and King's Shilling closely as they left the stable yard by way of the back gate.

"Well, her real name was Miss Hatchard, like the bookstore, but we pretended to be incapable of pronouncing it. Anyway, her methods were suited to the name Hatchet. She used a ruler to great advantage. She broke any number of them over my knuckles, especially when it came to handwriting."

"You were not an easy pupil," said Garrett, laughing as he listened to her tale, but wondering about this close relationship his ward had enjoyed—still enjoyed—with Price Matthews. He felt a twinge of . . . unease, he supposed it was, at the thought of Price's and Missy's pasts so unequivocally intertwined.

"That is putting it mildly. My mother despaired over my ever learning to read, though sums came easily to me."

"But you finally learned," said Garrett, bringing his gelding up alongside now that they were riding through open fields.

Missy cast him a quizzical glance and said, "Of

course. I manage to read anything I have to, though I still cannot abide wading through those dry sermons meant to improve a lady's mind, as Miss Hatchet was wont to say."

"So what do you read? Other than the racing news," he teased.

"I sometimes read novels," she confessed.

"Novels! I am aghast!" exclaimed Garrett.

"Laugh if you must, but they are quite entertaining," said Missy defiantly.

"I know. I read them all the time. I enjoy Miss Austen's, of course. I mean, one must, mustn't one?" said Garrett. Then, looking around furtively, he leaned closer and whispered, "But the ones I really enjoy are from the Minerva Press." He sat back again, his posture daring her to poke fun at him.

Missy giggled and admitted, "They are my favorite! Utterly impossible and utterly irresistible!"

"That sums it up quite nicely," said Garrett, grinning in return. "I know I am not supposed to like the blasted things. I mean, a man—a soldier at that—isn't supposed to like all that rubbish."

"How on earth did you get started reading them?" she asked.

"One of the other officers' wives was traveling with us. She had friends send them to her from home. I teased her about them one time too many, and she forced me to read one. I was hooked from then on. Several of us were, if you must know, but I am sworn to secrecy," he added, lowering his voice in a suitably stealthy tone.

"Now you are roasting me," she said.

"Word of a Wyndridge," he said, crossing his heart.

They continued along in companionable silence for a few more minutes before Missy asked suddenly, "Does Mr. Emery read them?"

"As his best friend, I cannot say."

"Then he does?" she persisted.

Garrett clamped his lips firmly together and refused to speak. Missy let out a whoop of laughter that sent King's Shilling crab-stepping to one side so that she had to grab the pommel.

"That's what you get for prying," said Garrett, one supercilious brow raised.

"Then you shouldn't tease me with such delicious gossip," said Missy, cocking her head to one side as they rode along and studying his chiseled profile.

After a moment, he turned, regarding her with the same frank curiosity. Her eyes fell under such scrutiny, and she suggested, "We should quit dawdling. I invited Price and his mother for supper; at this rate, they will be there before we are." She pressed her knees and sent King's Shilling cantering across the meadow, leaving a puzzled guardian to follow in her wake.

Missy was dressed in one of her oldest gowns for dinner; her better ones had been taken to London and discarded after her new wardrobe had been finished. For the first time, however, she keenly felt the lack of something more stylish, more flattering. She told her reflection that she had simply been spoiled by all the trappings of London; even if that was true, she admitted she missed her beautiful new gowns,

missed the admiring glances sent her way when she
wore them.

"Vanity, thy name is woman," she quoted, sticking
out her tongue at her image before picking up the
brush and trying to bring her wayward hair into some
semblance of order.

She twisted the thick mass into a coil, but it sprang
free before she could put enough pins in it to secure
it. Gritting her teeth, she tried again, meeting with
little success.

Disgusted, she released the heavy mane. Without
Felicity's help or Dulcie's talented hands, she could
do nothing. Picking up a lavender ribbon, Missy
threaded it beneath the long curls, brought it to the
top of her head, and tied a small bow. Running
the brush through the dark curls one last time, she
grunted with satisfaction. It was not *à la mode,* of
course, and she looked perhaps sixteen years old,
but it would have to do.

Missy opened the door and collided with a solid
object.

"Missy! How pretty you look tonight," said Garrett,
pulling his own door closed.

"What a corker," she said with a good-natured
laugh.

"But you do," he insisted. Beneath her disbelieving
grimace, he wavered and added, "Not in your usual
style, perhaps, but very pretty just the same. I like
your hair like that."

Missy let it pass, murmuring politely, "You are too
kind, sir."

He offered his arm, and they went down to dinner
together. Price Matthews and his mother were ex-

changing a few words with McMann in the hall when they descended the stairs. As Price eyed his old friend's sparkling eyes and glowing complexion, he exchanged a knowing nod with the old butler.

"Good evening, Matthews," said Garrett, extending his hand.

"Sir Garrett," he said. "Missy, I'm sorry I missed you this afternoon. Sir Garrett, may I present my mother, Mrs. Matthews."

"How do you do, madam?"

"Very well, thank you, Sir Garrett. My, Price didn't tell me how very handsome you were," said the older woman, her eyes traveling from Garrett to Missy and back again.

Garrett smiled but said nothing.

"Shall we go into the drawing room until dinner is ready?" suggested Missy, taking Mrs. Matthews's arm and leading her away.

The two men followed. With the ease of family, Price went to the old table by the fireplace and poured out drinks for everyone.

"To Lambert Farms," he said, holding his glass high.

"And to the handsome new owner," said Mrs. Matthews, taking another sip. Missy and Price followed suit, but Garrett only smiled.

"Tell me, Sir Garrett, where is your family from? I used to know some Wyndridges, but it was ages ago, when I was a girl."

"We're from Hampshire, near Wynchester."

"No, couldn't be the same ones. Perhaps a distant connection of some sort. Tell me, Sir Garrett, how do you like Yorkshire so far?"

"It is quite beautiful," said Garrett. "I'm looking forward to living here."

"And you, Missy—will you live in the dower house? It will take quite a bit of work to make it habitable again," said Mrs. Matthews.

"I . . . suppose . . ."

"Missy will be staying here as long as she likes, Mrs. Matthews. This is her home, and I am her guardian, though that formal relationship will end in a year or two."

Mrs. Matthews opened her mouth to speak, but her son forestalled her, saying smoothly, "There, you see, Mother. I told you we wouldn't be losing Missy. Ah, here is McMann to announce dinner.

Price stepped forward and offered his arm to his mother. Grudgingly, the older woman accepted and was led in to dinner. Garrett tucked Missy's hand into the crook of his arm, favoring her with a wry smile and nodding toward Mrs. Matthews with a raised brow.

"She means well," whispered Missy.

"Thank heavens," he replied.

Garrett sat at the head of the table with Mrs. Matthews on his right. Missy was at the foot with Price on her right. With such a small gathering, the table had been shortened to its smallest size to allow for general conversation.

"The problem, as I see it, Sir Garrett," began Mrs. Matthews as soon as they were settled, "is not so much what works at the moment, but what will work in the future. Have you thought what will happen in a household with two mistresses?" She speared a brussels sprout and chomped into it with relish.

"I'm afraid I don't understand, Mrs. Matthews. There aren't two mistresses here."

"Ah, but there will be when you take a wife, as you'll no doubt be thinking about doing soon. You aren't getting any younger. As I am always telling Price, it is well past time to set up his nursery."

"Mother!" "Aunt Sylvia!" "Mrs. Matthews!" came the chorus of reactions.

"Mother, you are being outrageous again," said her son, a warning in his voice.

"Nonsense; I am only stating facts."

"Then be so kind as to keep your facts to yourself," said Price indignantly.

"Please, Aunt Sylvia," begged Missy.

The little old woman studied each of them in turn before she grunted and shrugged, saying, "Very well. As long as you're thinking about it."

"I assure you, Mrs. Matthews, we shan't forget your warning," said Garrett. He signaled the footman to come forward. "Would you care for some more wine?"

Dinner progressed without further contretemps. Mrs. Matthews, who considered herself a moving force in the neighborhood, quizzed Garrett on his plans for everything from the Christmas baskets for the poor to the continuation of the Autumn Festival.

"Tell me about the festival," he said, happy to have a safe topic to fill their conversation.

"It is held every year here at Lambert Farm. Everyone brings something, from the smallest child to Mr. Yancy, who is near one hundred years old. The gentry and the workers celebrate the harvest, side by side, with dancing and games. It's a grand time."

"And don't forget the races, Mother. That's the best part, isn't it, Missy? Do you remember the three-legged race last year?"

"I remember you knocked me down!" she said, laughing. "We still could have won if you had only leaned on my shoulder."

"Leaned on your shoulder?" asked Garrett, his palm beginning to itch as he put on a polite smile for his audience.

"Yes, we entered together. You know, you tie two of your legs together to make a third leg."

"Price fell over just in front of the finish line."

"I twisted my ankle," he protested.

"But I could have supported you," said Missy. "He was too busy laughing," she added for Garrett's benefit.

"How unsporting of you, Matthews. Couldn't you wait until after the race to give in to the pain?" said Garrett.

"That's what Missy thinks, but she would do anything to win! Only call it a competition of some sort, and there's no limit to what she will do to win," said Price, smiling at his old friend in an intimate way that made Garrett want to pummel his face.

"I can't help it," Missy protested, reaching out and patting Price's hand.

Garrett cleared his throat. Or was it a growl? He turned to Mrs. Matthews and asked, "What other time-honored traditions do you have here?"

When the last bite of trifle had been consumed, and the ladies had adjourned to the drawing room, Garrett offered Price a glass of port and said, "I don't want to talk business tonight, but I was wondering if you could make yourself available in the morning."

"Certainly. What time?"

"Shall we say nine o'clock?"

"I'll be here," said Price, glancing toward the door.

Garrett interpreted his guest's expression as yearning, and he suggested they join the ladies. When they entered the drawing room, Missy was playing the pianoforte while Mrs. Matthews had pulled out her knitting from someplace and her needles were clicking away busily.

Garrett sat down close to the pianoforte and closed his eyes. He awoke when the music stopped, and McMann was wheeling in the tea tray.

"I beg your pardon. I am not usually so rude. I suppose the past few days have finally caught up with me."

"Think nothing of it, my boy," said Mrs. Matthews, putting away her knitting and patting the seat beside her on the overstuffed sofa. "Come sit here, and I'll pour you a nice cup of tea."

Like a little boy, Garrett did as she bade him. The hot liquid revived him, and he soon felt wide awake—awake enough to notice Price and Missy seated in matching chairs, side by side, talking so quietly he couldn't hear them.

Mrs. Matthews, also looking on the pair, said fondly, "They have always been so close. I still hope, you know, they will one day come to their senses and make a match of it."

"Do you?" said Garrett coolly.

"Oh, yes; they are perfect for each other. Although I must confess, Sir Garrett," she said, winking at him,

'when I saw you coming down the stairs with Missy
on your arm, I did wonder if perhaps . . ."

"But?" he prompted.

"But now I can see you are no threat to my hope
for dear Price. I know he has asked her several times,
but she has always turned him down. Maybe this
time . . ."

Maybe this time? thought Garrett, grinding his teeth
as he watched Missy lean forward and brush a crumb
from Price's shoulder. She bent her head to listen to
some whispered confidence, then giggled. Both of
them giggled.

Garrett stood up abruptly and said, "I am sorry to
have to leave this delightful company, but I really am
worn out. I suppose I must bid you good night, Mrs.
Matthews."

He bowed over the matron's hand and paused,
looking at Price and Missy, waiting for them to rise
and follow his lead. When they didn't, he merely
bowed in their direction, mumbled "good night,"
and stalked out of the room.

"What on earth did you say to the man, Mother?"
demanded Price.

"Why, nothing at all. Do tell Cook how wonderful
these biscuits are, Missy," said Mrs. Matthews, smiling
contentedly.

"Certainly," she replied, her gaze straying to the
door through which Garrett had just passed.

Garrett gave a nod of approval when Price Matthews presented himself at the study promptly the
next morning.

"Come in, Matthews. Have a seat. A cup of coffee too, if you like."

"Thank you, Sir Garrett. I trust you are feeling rested this morning," said Price, making himself comfortable.

"Wha—oh, yes, quite," said Garrett, unwilling to admit to his bailiff, Missy's friend, that he had lain awake forever listening for her footstep in the hall, for her door to open and close. He had listened for the bumps and creaks that signaled her getting ready for bed, until finally silence had fallen in the house.

Even then, it had taken him another hour to find sleep. But he could only barely admit this to himself; he certainly wasn't ready to advertise the fact.

"What can I do for you this morning?" prompted Price after several minutes had passed and his new employer still had not spoken.

"Oh, yes; I want you to take a look at these," said Garrett, pushing the ledgers across the old desk.

Price opened to the first page of entries and grunted knowingly.

"I know everyone has their own system, Matthews, but I need to understand yours in order to read these things. For instance, what does 'E, 0, T, S' mean?"

Price shook his head, grimacing in concentration. Garrett began to frown as Price pushed the books back across the desk and sat back.

"I'm afraid I can't help you. I never have been able to decipher Missy's writing. Not this kind of writing. She does all right with letters and such, but there's just not enough to go on with these abbreviated entries. You'll just have to ask Missy."

Garrett's frown grew. He opened the ledgers again. Pointing at the page, he said, "You mean to tell me Missy wrote all this?"

"Of course," said Price.

"But how did she know what to write? I mean, the person who keeps the ledgers is the person who runs the show."

"Now you understand," said Price, beginning to grin at Garrett in the most infuriating manner.

"So you are telling me that all this time since her father's death, Miss Mystique Lambert has been running Lambert Farm?"

"Not all of it. I take care of the tenants, the crops, the livestock, except the horses. Missy did the rest. And I don't think I would let her hear me calling her Mystique. She really can't abide that name."

"But how can a slip of a girl do all that?"

"She just did. Even before her father died, before he even got sick, Missy was taking over. She didn't go to all the races, but her father let her have free rein here, deciding which mares to buy, which stallion to pair with which mare."

"I don't believe it," said Garrett, but he was beginning to realize the enormity of the underestimation of Missy.

"You should, Sir Garrett. There is more to Missy Lambert than a striking face. She is Lambert Farm."

Bemused, Garrett dismissed his bailiff, turning his chair around so it faced the open window of the study. He finally focused on the old stone barn at the foot of the hill, and he grinned.

* * *

Missy sat on a table in the tack room, her heels swinging to and fro as she watched Roberts mend a bridle. In the house, in her study, Garrett had once more closeted himself with Price, "going over the books."

"Why are some people so dim-witted?" she asked.

Roberts looked up from his work, grinning, and said, "Some people? Or one in particular?"

"You know who I mean, and I shouldn't have said such a thing. Please do not regard it, Roberts," she added, her legs starting to swing again. "But you know it is really very difficult to be charitable when a person won't even listen."

"Have you told him, Lady Miss? Have you told him flat out that you're the brains behind Lambert racing and have been for five years or more?"

"I tried, but I couldn't make him believe me."

"Don't worry; he'll come around. Otherwise he'll never learn anything about the operation. When he started in on me, I couldn't answer his questions. I suggested he talk to you, but . . ."

"He wouldn't listen," she finished for him.

Missy hopped down from the table and picked up the tack for Angel, one of the older mares.

"If anyone wants me, I'm going for a ride," she said.

"I'll tell him, Lady Miss," said Roberts, beginning to whistle tunelessly.

Missy and Angel traveled at a leisurely pace across the meadow and down to the small pond. The sun was hot, and there was no breeze. Missy felt a trickle of perspiration dampen her shirt. She slipped to the ground, leaving the mare to graze without being tethered down.

Removing her shoes and stockings, she was sorely tempted to undress completely and slip into the cool, clear water. But she was there for a purpose, waiting for Garrett, though she wasn't convinced he would show up.

Even if Price could convince him that she was the only one who could explain the breeding and racing management, she wasn't sure he would come to her. After all, how well did she know Sir Garrett Wyndridge? Was he the sort of man who would accept help from a woman?

"Missy?"

She looked toward the opening in the clearing where Garrett was outlined by the bright sun.

"Missy, I need your help."

Nine

Missy's nose crinkled as she frowned at the next entry. She held it away from her, tilting her head to one side, trying to get a different perspective on the scrawled lettering.

"It certainly looks like 'E-O-T-S,'" she said. "But it couldn't be. That doesn't mean a thing to me. Wait a minute! Now I remember. That was from last winter when we ran short of feed. I bought some oats from the Edwardses' estate. That's 'E' for Edwards, and the other is actually 'oats.' See the little bump? That's the 'a,'" she said triumphantly.

"How in the world am I supposed to be able to read your code, Missy, if I can't even read the letters?" complained Garrett.

She shrugged, saying haughtily, "Really, I don't see that it matters so much with one small entry."

"But how am I to know that 'KN' refers to Lord Knight's stud fees or that the 'E' is for Edwards?"

Missy relented, suggesting, "I suppose I could go through and make a list of all the abbreviations I used. I'm afraid my handwriting has never been very legible. I am sorry, Garrett. I did try to keep better books for you . . . well, for the heir, at any rate."

"I appreciate that, Missy. I'm sorry to be such a bear. It's just that there is so much to learn and so much to remember. I'm beginning to despair of ever learning all I need to know," said Garrett, pushing away from the desk where he had drawn up a chair next to Missy's.

They had spent the entire afternoon going over all the ledgers, with Garrett making extensive notes about the cost of feed and supplies, the income from racing and from stud fees. Now he picked up his notes and pitched them across the battered desk with a muffled curse and rose, stretching his stiff muscles.

Missy grinned up at him and said, "This is the time when I would always head for the stables and saddle the first horse I came to and ride until time to dress for dinner."

"That sounds like a winner! Shall we?"

"Wonderful!" she said, staring for a moment at the hand he had extended before taking it and rising. They walked hand in hand to the door before Garrett fell back to allow her to precede him into the hall.

In no time, they were racing across the meadow, not slowing until they had lost sight of the house and barns. Finally they slowed their mounts to a desultory walk, enjoying the cool quiet of the late afternoon as the sun sank lower on the horizon.

"Missy, what do you plan to do after the Season? I mean, if you haven't, er, formed an attachment," he added, not daring to look at her.

"Oh, I don't know. I expect Felicity will have settled on one of her beaux, so there will be the wedding to plan and all the bride clothes and such."

"Do you think she has a favorite?" asked Garrett.

"I think she likes Mr. Cholmes well enough. And then there is also Lord Fallworth. He has been quite particular in his attentions."

"Then you think she is over her infatuation with Ian?"

"I think that is safe to say," said Missy with a laugh. "My sister is very sweet-natured; she rarely allows anyone or anything to make her angry, but Mr. Emery managed to do so quite nicely. I don't think she will soon forgive him."

"It's for the best. So we have Felicity taken care of. What of you? You know you are welcome to make your home here for as long as you wish, no matter what Mrs. Matthews says about it," said Garrett, turning in his saddle to face her.

"Thank you, Garrett. I appreciate that. And I probably will want to come back for a time, at least while the dower house is being refurbished. At least I would be on hand to help you learn your way around," she added, trying her best to sound buoyant, but fearing she was failing miserably.

"True, but I don't mean to be selfish about it. You must live your own life, of course. You must feel free to go to London for the Season, to visit Felicity, and so on."

"That is very good of you, Garrett," she said quietly.

"Missy," he said.

"Yes?"

"I have to ask. Why are you helping me?" he asked, stopping his horse.

Missy pulled up also and said, "I don't understand what you mean, Garrett."

"It occurred to me that, were I in your shoes, I might be tempted to stand back and let the person who usurped my birthright drown in his own proud ignorance. But you didn't. You even forgave me for being a pompous ass, asking everyone but you for help. How can you be so good? So forgiving?"

Missy grinned at him. "I was tempted, sorely tempted. But you know why I can't let you fail."

"I'm not sure," he admitted.

"I love Lambert Farm too much to see it destroyed. You know, horseracing is a risky business even for someone who has been reared to it. It's not like a big estate. With that, you can make some bad choices and still survive. But in the breeding business, you can't afford to make stupid mistakes."

"And I would have," said Garrett humbly. "I nearly did already. I almost let you slip through my fingers," he added softly.

Startled, Missy's gaze flew to his face. He was looking down at her tenderly. Or was that the soft light of the setting sun? she wondered wildly.

"But you didn't," she whispered.

Garrett lifted one hand to stroke her cheek and said, "That is one thing I did right. I must admit, I . . ."

He frowned as he heard someone shouting in the distance. Swiveling around, he watched as two approaching riders continued to shout his name. "What the devil?"

Missy heard one of the riders yell her sister's name, and she whirled her horse around, urging the mare forward to meet the men. Garrett was right by her side.

"Lady Miss! Sir Garrett! Major, sir!" called Putty, his voice hoarse from shouting.

"Easy, man, you'll be fainting in a minute," advised ever unruffled Roberts, pulling up beside the trio. "Sir Garrett, Mr. Putty just arrived, and as he said it was urgent, I thought I should bring him out to meet with you."

"Thank you, Roberts."

"Putty, what is it? Miss Felicity . . . ?" said Missy, her face ashen with fear. Garrett put his hand over hers.

The giant shook his head, unable to meet her eye.

Garrett barked, "Out with it, man!"

Still reluctant, the servant eyed Roberts.

"Just tell me, Putty," urged Missy. "I would trust Roberts with my life."

"It's Miss Felicity. She's run away."

"Run away?" breathed Missy, incredulous. "That's impossible! Felicity would never do such a thing!"

"Putty, are you sure?"

"That's what Mr. Turtle told me to tell you. He told me to ride to Yorkshire as if my life depended on it and tell you about Miss Felicity," said Putty.

"But why?" asked Missy.

"With whom?" demanded Garrett.

"Mr. Turtle wasn't sure, sir. There was a note that Miss Angelica showed to Miss Dill. Right there in front of Mr. Turtle, but he didn't get a look at it. He seemed to think it might be Mr. Emery!"

But this news was too ludicrous to consider sensible, and Garrett said, "Wait a minute. You rode all this way because Turtle overhead Miss Angelica gossiping about Miss Felicity to Miss Dill?"

Listening to Garrett restored Missy's sense of balance, and she met his wink with a tiny smile.

"But Mr. Turtle told me she was missing," said Putty.

"Oh, Garrett," breathed Missy. "This would never have happened if I had stayed in London as you wished."

"Sh! It's not your fault," said Garrett, hoping she would not be so imprudent as to mention their irregular journey to Yorkshire.

"Look, we will leave first thing in the morning. I'm sure when we reach London, we will discover this is all a hum," began Garrett, watching Missy's eyes fill with tears and wishing he could take her in his arms to comfort her.

"But Mr. Turtle said—"

"Never mind, Putty. You ride ahead with Roberts. Tell them to put dinner forward. We will need an early night if we are to make London in two days."

When they were alone, Garrett once again reached out and placed his hand over Missy's, squeezing her hand in a bracing manner.

"Don't worry. Everything will be fine. Just wait and see."

"I do hope you're right, Garrett," she said, but the look she gave him was not hopeful.

Throughout dinner, Missy tried to keep up her end of the conversation, but it was forced, and soon Garrett gave up. They fell into a morose silence.

Missy couldn't imagine her sister so lost to propriety that she would elope with a man! And which man?

Because surely it wasn't Mr. Emery. Felicity held him in contempt.

Then another worry assailed Missy. What if Felicity hadn't eloped? What if the man was merely tricking her and was going to take advantage of her?

"Garrett, I'm afraid," she said, her voice almost a whisper.

"Don't be. It is probably nothing like Turtle and Putty think," said Garrett with more confidence than he felt.

"But what if she has been duped by some unscrupulous man who only has plans to ruin her? I mean, a Gretna Green marriage would be bad enough, but what if Felicity was taken in by some man's honeyed words."

"Nonsense! You know Felicity better than that. And besides, how would this unscrupulous fellow gain access to her in the first place? Dillie wouldn't allow it!"

Missy found little comfort in his words. They both knew that Dillie was often too wrapped up in her own affairs to notice whom her charges were flirting with.

"Shall I clear, Lady Miss?" asked McMann, his voice shaky and his eyes bright with unshed tears. Word of Felicity's downfall had spread like wildfire through the household staff.

"Yes, please. And, McMann, please apologize to Cook for us. I'm afraid we didn't do her dinner justice."

"Very good, miss.

"And never mind about tea tonight, McMann. We want to get an early start in the morning. We won't stay up for tea," said Garrett, rising and escorting Missy out of the dining room.

"I think I'll just have one glass of brandy before bed, Missy. Would you care to join me?" he asked.

She shook her head.

"It might help you sleep," said Garrett.

Missy managed a smile for him and said, "No thank you, Garrett. I don't think I could keep it down. I'll see you bright and early in the morning."

"Very well. I hope to leave by eight o'clock."

Missy looked like her old determined self when she said, "Make it seven. It will be daylight by then."

"Seven it is. Good night, my dear. Do get some sleep."

"I'll try. Good night, Garrett."

Missy climbed the stairs with measured tread. She knew that sleep, if it came at all, would be elusive. She almost turned back to join Garrett, but the sweet agony of spending one last evening with him, in private, would unravel her carefully marshaled composure completely.

She laid out her gown for the journey, another of her old dresses which had seen better days several years past. Oh, well, that was what she got for stowing away in the boot of a carriage. She dressed for bed and wandered to the window where the grounds and barns were painted in the glowing light of the full moon.

Only this afternoon, she had been content with life. Garrett had shown her that he truly respected her opinions, her skills. They had begun a new camaraderie, born of his need for her knowledge, of course, not from any warmer feelings.

When they were alone riding, however, she had wondered if perhaps, just perhaps, he was coming to care for her a little. At the very least, he had to acknowledge she was proving more helpful than he ever imagined. Had he listened to her back in London, she would not have been forced to stow away in his carriage.

And Felicity might have been prevented from making the biggest mistake of her life! moaned Missy, walking to the bed and throwing herself on it facedown.

A few moments later, she sat up, legs crossed, and leaned over, retrieving her book from the nightstand. It was an old novel she had read several times. She never tired of the part where the hero rescued the heroine, throwing her over the pommel of his saddle and carrying her away.

It was too bad real life wasn't like that, thought Missy, opening the book once again.

It was a nightmare that woke her, writhing against the confines of the blankets, tears forcing their way from closed lids, her teeth chattering with fear. She had tried to cry out, to beg for . . . but the dream was already fading, and the last thing Missy wanted was to make it begin again.

She threw the covers off and sprang out of bed, restless and unhappy, but incapable of identifying the cause. The dream wasn't new; it had come to her several times after her father's death, after the reading of his will, when she had learned that Lambert Farm would not be hers.

Shivering, Missy hurried to the wardrobe and

pulled out a clean pair of breeches and a heavy shirt. She dressed hurriedly, some unseen power urging her toward the stables as if to warn her it was her last chance.

Her racing pulse slowed as she reached the old barn and took a deep breath. Her heart regained its regular rhythm by the time she reached King's stall.

He pushed against her, and she whispered, "I'm sorry, sweeting. I didn't stop to pick up a treat. I was too anxious to see you. We have to talk."

The big horse shook his head and moved to his feed trough to search for elusive feed.

Missy picked up a curry brush and began taking long strokes against the glossy chestnut rump, chatting with him all the while.

"You see, King, we have arrived at a juncture in our lives. I know you are still very frightened . . ." She chuckled when he snorted, as if to deny her allegation. Missy continued, "Yes, well, perhaps frightened is not the right word. Shall we say skittish? Yes, skittish is better."

She moved up to his neck. "You see, I have to return to London in the morning. It would be a marvelous chance for you to prove yourself, to prove you are ready to be sociable. We already know you are the fastest horse in the kingdom," she added, to placate him.

"So, I know it may be a little soon, but I really want you to go with me. You'll have a chance to grow accustomed to all the hubbub there. Then, when it is time to run, to show all the world your speed, you'll be ready."

"Lady Miss? Is that you?" asked Putty, holding a

lantern high and craning to see if it was really Missy in King's stall.

"Yes, it is. I hope I didn't disturb you, Putty. You should be asleep. You've ridden all day, and you're about to turn around and do the same again," said Missy, walking around the stallion and joining the servant at the door of the stall, turning to watch King's Shilling.

"I couldn't sleep. I know I'll be sorry tomorrow but I just couldn't. I guess you couldn't either," said the kindly giant.

"I'm afraid not. I am worried about my sister, certainly, but there is more to it than that." Missy turned and studied Putty's profile. King had moved over to the door and was allowing Putty to scratch him behind the ear.

"That's odd," she murmured.

"Oh, he's a sweet thing, is King. When I visited before, he and I got t' be the best o' friends."

"You did?" she asked.

"Yes, ma'am. He's a nice fellow. Roberts told me as how he's a terror around the other grooms, but we get along just fine. Maybe it's because we're both so big."

Missy opened the door and slipped outside. "Will he let you handle him?" she asked, incredulous.

"I suppose. I mean, I haven't spent that much time with him, but . . . That's a good boy," said Putty, taking King by the halter and leading him out of the stall, down the row and back again. "He doesn't seem to mind."

The stallion butted against his back, and Putty

aughed. He reached into his pocket and pulled out
peppermint candy.

"He really likes these things."

"Putty, this is wonderful! You're wonderful," said
Missy. "Do you think he would allow you to ride
im?"

"Oh, I don't know. I could try. I don't think he
ould take exception to it; I'm too big for him to
hrow."

"Try it," said Missy breathlessly.

She watched in awe as Putty swung up easily. King's
hilling rolled his head around and blew on Putty's
eg, but he didn't shy or rear up.

"Putty, this is amazing!" said Missy. Using only his
nees, Putty guided the stallion down to the far end
f the barn, turning him easily and bringing him
ack to Missy's side.

"I worked with the horses in the army," he ex-
lained. "They seem to like my company."

"Putty, do you think you could ride King's Shilling
ll the way to London? I mean, I would help if Sir
Garrett doesn't take exception to the idea."

"I don't think he'd be very happy in London,
niss."

"But I need for him to settle down if I am ever to
ace him, Putty. And I need desperately to race him,"
he added, her hopes and heart in her eyes.

The gentle giant was not proof against it. He
greed.

The ride back to London was grueling. Garrett and
eth alternated driving, and Putty rode King's Shil-

ling. There had been a knock-down-and-drag-out be
fore Garrett had finally agreed to allow King's Shil
ling to tag along. In the end, it had been Missy'
proud announcement that the decision was only her
to make, since King's Shilling was her personal horse

So Garrett had agreed, although he had forbidden
her to ride the edgy stallion in case he should decide
to bolt. For her part, Missy had been satisfied. So sh
rode inside the carriage, holding on tight and trying
not to complain as her body was jostled and bruise
by the punishing pace Garrett set.

The first evening, they finally stopped at the sam
inn where they had stayed on the way to Yorkshire
Garrett pulled into the yard, never considering tha
when he had headed north, he had not had a "sis
ter." This time, he not only required an extra room
for his sister, but she bore an amazing resemblanc
to one of his grooms. Only Garrett's barking of or
ders prevented the landlord from inquiring any fur
ther into the matter.

Missy climbed the stairs to her room and stripped
off the worn gown, slipping into her nightrail and a
thin wrapper just in time before Garrett was knocking
on her door.

"I thought you might like some tea and a bite to
eat before retiring, sister mine," he said, entering the
tiny room and placing a tray on the dresser.

"I don't know if I can stay awake that long," said
Missy, closing the door and sitting on the edge of the
bed while he served her.

"I know, but we will leave very early. There won'
be much time for a proper breakfast, and I don'
want it said I starved my sister," he said, grinning

down at her before returning to the tray and pouring a cup of tea for himself. "You don't mind if I join you, do you? I just couldn't face that empty private parlor tonight."

"Of course not; do have a seat," replied Missy, tugging at her wrapper so it covered her bare feet.

Garrett sat down in the only chair and began devouring the sandwiches on his plate. Missy nibbled at hers, wishing she could think of something witty to say.

"I know one thing. I hope I never have to make a trip like this again," said Garrett. "I didn't think I was that old until today. I'm quite burnt to the socket."

"So am I," said Missy, taking cover behind her teacup.

"I do believe I could sleep around the clock," he added.

"Yes, yes," she murmured, cursing herself for a ninnyhammer. Really! She was acting like a schoolgirl.

"You're exhausted," said Garrett, rising and taking the cup from her unresisting hands. "I shouldn't have disturbed you just because I wanted company."

"No, Garrett, I don't mind. And I appreciate the tea tray. Really," said Missy, covering her mouth as she yawned.

Garrett leaned forward and kissed her forehead. "Good night, sister."

"Good night, Garrett," Missy stammered—after the door had closed behind him.

Wide awake now, Missy climbed into bed to spend the next few hours in a sea of confusion. When sleep

finally came, in her dreams she relived Garrett's kiss.
Not exactly the same chaste kiss of reality, but when
Missy awoke the next morning and compared the
two, the kiss of her dreams won the contest, without
a doubt.

The journey almost over, Missy's mind turned
from her state of discomfort and confusion to the
problem of her sister's elopement. How she hoped
Garrett would be proven right, that it was all a hum.
But something warned her that such was not the
case.

Garrett turned the ribbons over to his groom and
joined Missy inside the carriage. Too weary for words,
Missy fell into a restless sleep, her head resting
against Garrett's arm.

They drove directly into the stable yard, Garrett
wanting to avoid any inquisitive eyes that might be
interested in their entourage. Though Missy was his
ward, their riding in a closed carriage together
might be viewed in an unfavorable light, especially
if anyone inquired closely about the length of their
journey.

Missy was torn between rushing into the house and
demanding the latest news about Felicity and seeing
to the needs of her horse.

Putty set her mind at ease, saying, "Run along,
Lady Miss. I'll take care of King. Don't you worry
about him for a minute."

"Thank you, Putty. You're a dear." She patted the
stallion's nose and hurried away, missing out on the
rosy blush that spread across the servant's face.

* * *

"Sir Garrett! Thank heavens you have come home," said Turtle dramatically when he saw his master enter the hall.

"Where is Miss Dill?" he demanded, not pausing to remove his coat and hat but going directly into the drawing room, Missy and the butler on his heels.

"Cousin Garrett!" exclaimed Dillie, who dropped her knitting, and Angelica, who jumped up, sending a sheet of paper floating to the floor. She hurriedly retrieved it and shoved it into her bosom.

"Where is she?" demanded Garrett.

"Who?" they asked in unison.

"Who?" echoed Garrett. "Felicity, of course!"

"Why, she isn't here right now. She has gone out of town," said Dillie. "We weren't expecting you, or I am certain Felicity would have planned to be here for your homecoming. Do sit down and tell us all about your trip. And, Missy, naughty thing, you should have warned me you were going with Cousin Garrett. I was so surprised when I read your note."

"Dillie, we have been frantic with worry about Felicity," said Missy. "Where is she?"

"Why, I told you. She went out of town. But why would you be worried about her? I'm sure it is not so unusual for a betrothed couple to visit future in-laws."

Missy grabbed Garrett's arm for support, and he led her to the nearest chair before ordering the hovering Turtle to fetch a glass of sherry.

"Betrothed," she whispered, looking stricken.

Garrett turned his blazing green eyes on the hapless Dillie who was still smiling. Before he could speak, however, the door to the drawing room opened and Felicity, glowing with happiness, sailed into the room.

She paused in midstep, taking in the tableau with ever widening eyes. Turning, she held out her hand to Ian Emery, who stepped forward, a big smile fixed firmly on his face.

"Hullo, Garrett," he said, extending his free hand to his old friend. Numbly, Garrett shook it. "Sorry we didn't wait for your permission, but I knew Mother was going to be visiting my other sister in Hampstead, and I did want to introduce her to my fiancée before she returned to Bath. I knew you would approve anyway, so we went ahead and sent the notice to the papers and all." Ian paused, looking from one member of the ensemble to the next. Frowning, he added, "You do approve, don't you?"

"Felicity, a word with you in private, if you please," said Garrett, ignoring his friend and leading the way to his study. Missy and Felicity hurried after him.

When the door was closed, Missy cried, "Why, Felicity? Why would you wish to ally yourself with this man . . . this rake?"

Her younger sister held herself proudly; looking down her nose at Missy, she said, "Why? Because I love him, that's why, Missy. You may not understand, but I had hoped you would respect my wishes. And you, Garrett. You may be my guardian, but until six weeks ago, I had never seen you before. How can you dare to deny me the right to choose my own husband?"

Garrett began to chuckle, and he leaned forward and took Felicity's trembling hand in his, lifting it to his mouth for a chaste kiss.

"I wouldn't dare deny you that right, Felicity," he said. "You may have to convince your sister, but you have my blessing. I think you're much too good for Ian, but then, I daresay you will soon have him whipped into shape."

"Thank you, Garrett," said Felicity, dimpling up at him. She turned to her sister. "Missy?"

Missy was visibly torn, but she said, "If you're sure . . ."

Felicity nodded, and Missy threw her arms around her sister's neck. Amid happy tears, they rejoined the others. Ian Emery shook his friend's hand, wincing slightly at the firmness of the grip.

"Word of a Wyndridge: If you do anything to betray that sweet child . . ." Garrett said quietly, beneath the cover of all the congratulations.

"That sweet child is a tower of strength, Garrett, but I will do nothing to betray her trust in me. I promise."

"Then welcome to the family."

Garrett ordered champagne for everyone in the household, and they drank toasts to the happy couple. When the servants had been dismissed, Garrett motioned to the butler to stay behind.

"Turtle," he said quietly, "next time, please get your facts straight. I appreciate your sending for me, but it would have been a much more leisurely journey had we known the truth."

"Of course, Sir Garrett. My profound apologies," added the discomfited butler.

"Never mind. It is forgotten. After all, we have succeeded in marrying off, and quite well, one of our charges. Only two more to go," said Garrett.

Gratified, the butler smiled and confided, "I thin
Miss Wyndridge may soon have some news for you
too. She has been receiving flowers and letters from
the same gentleman every day for a week."

"And who is the gentleman?" asked Garrett with
a frown. He didn't think he liked his wards having
secrets from him. Two months ago, he wouldn't have
thought twice about it, but now, with the responsibility weighing heavily on his shoulders, he worried
about their choices.

The butler shook his head. "That, I couldn't say
The notes are always written in the same hand, but
they are merely signed, 'an admirer.' "

"I see. Thank you, Turtle. That will be all."

Garrett rejoined the ladies and Ian, but he was pre
occupied and promised himself he would have a few
words in private with Angelica at the first opportunity

Really, it had been selfish and foolish of him to
leave his wards in London, unprotected and practically unchaperoned. While Dillie's presence offered
the girls added respectability, and they obviously
adored her, she did not always show good judgment
He would be more attentive in the future.

His eyes softened as his gaze fell on Missy. She
looked weary; there were dark circles under her eyes
but she was smiling. What a trouper she was! All tha
way in only two days, and she never complained. I
ever a chap wanted a wife who could stand by hi
side, shoulder to shoulder. . . .

Garrett shied away from the thought, but he
couldn't tear his eyes away from her. She had severa
envelopes in her lap and was opening them, reading
them.

Garrett frowned. She was smiling—that thoughtful, sweet smile that signaled someone had given her a compliment. She smiled in just such a manner when he flattered her.

His frown deepened to a scowl. He had thought he could relax now that one of his charges was betrothed. He hadn't reckoned with worrying about Missy. Somehow, he hadn't seriously considered the possibility that she would marry. Or at least, marry someone else.

She chuckled at something in one of the letters; returning it to its envelope, she placed it in the pocket of her gown.

Just what the deuce was she reading? wondered Garrett. And, more importantly, just who the devil had written it?

Missy slept late the next morning, exhaustion finally taking its toll. When she did awake, she dressed hurriedly and made her way to the mews to check on King's Shilling. Putty had him out of his stall and was walking him around the small yard.

"He's so calm," she said, slipping the big horse a carrot and rubbing his face.

"Haven't seen a hint of a problem yet, Lady Miss. Maybe he was just bored up there in the country."

"I don't think so, Putty," said Missy. "Why don't you saddle him? I thought I would go for a ride."

"Sir Garrett would sack me for sure, miss. Please don't ask me to do that. Besides, King is tired today. Let's let him rest until tomorrow morning."

"I suppose that would be for the best," said Missy "I'm rather tired today myself."

"Thank you, miss," said the servant with a smile "What time in the morning?"

"Shall we say eight o'clock? I know that is terribl early by London standards, but I want to be in th park before there is too much excitement on th streets."

"Eight o'clock it is," he replied, turning and lead ing the stallion away.

Missy wandered back to the house. Her stomac growled, so she chose the kitchen door, leaving mo ments later with a small tray filled with all sorts o fare to tempt her appetite.

She made her way to the hall and surprised Turtle who was listening at the door to Garrett's study. No that he couldn't have heard just as well from nex door, at least what Angelica was shouting.

"I beg your pardon, miss," said the servant, spring ing away from the door as quickly as his old age per mitted.

"Quite a ruckus," commented Missy. "How long has it been going on?"

"Not above ten minutes. I believe Miss Wyndridge will shortly be—"

The door flew open and Angelica stormed pas Missy and Turtle without so much as a word. Tearing up the stairs, wailing at the top of her lungs, she dis appeared from sight. A few seconds later, they hear the door to her bedroom slam shut.

"As I was saying, Miss Wyndridge will shortly b going to her room," said the butler, tucking his hea down and sauntering off toward the kitchens.

Garrett, looking a little worn and tattered, came to the door of his study, gazing at Missy in a bemused sort of way.

"Would you care to share my bounty?" she asked, stepping past him and placing the tray on the table near the old leather sofa. "Pour yourself a drink, Garrett, and join me," she advised.

Garrett did as she bade and then dropped onto the sofa, his expression dark and foreboding.

"Is that anger or a pout?" asked Missy. When he responded only with a grunt, she added, "A pout, eh? She must have won the day."

He accepted a plate filled with cheese and ham and biscuits. "I suppose so. I discovered she was receiving secret correspondence from some man."

"How did you discover that?" asked Missy, popping a slice of juicy peach into her mouth.

"From Turtle," said Garrett. "I know, I know. His information about Felicity was less than helpful or accurate. But Turtle said this has been going on for over a week. I asked Angelica who was sending her all the letters and flowers, and she refused to tell me at first."

"Why? Is he so ineligible?"

"No. As it turns out, he is perfectly eligible, but the boy is a poet, a dilettante," explained Garrett, his expression turning to one of distaste.

"Boy? How old is he?" asked Missy.

"Twenty-four or so. He writes the worst poetry I have ever read," said Garrett.

"She allowed you to read her letters?" asked Missy, incredulous.

"Not exactly," said Garrett, trying to loosen his cravat, which had suddenly grown too tight. Coloring, he confessed, "I took the one that arrived this morning and read it before she came downstairs. Utter drivel. And he wants to marry her!"

"To marry her? That is serious," said Missy with a chuckle. "I don't know that I would allow such a thing, were I her guardian."

"You're making game of me," grumbled Garrett. "But I only have her best interest at heart."

"But it is *her* heart that matters," said Missy, wiping his chin as she would a child's. "You may think him an utter nuisance, but what you think doesn't matter. Can he support her?"

"She claims he is heir to a viscountcy and a vast estate to boot," Garrett revealed grudgingly.

"Then perhaps you should give your consent when, and if, he comes to call," she added sensibly. When he still did not agree, Missy smiled sweetly and said, "If you do accept his suit, only one to go."

"There is that," murmured Garrett. "Just promise me one thing, Missy. You won't choose some wet-behind-the-ears child with more hair than wit."

"That, I can safely promise you, Garrett," she said. "You must try this cheese. I don't know what it is, but we must have Cook buy more of it."

While she added some of the cheese to his plate, Garrett watched her, his tender smile growing in warmth.

Ten

Missy had planned to spend the remainder of the afternoon quietly reading, but Dulcie entered her room around four o'clock and handed her a small envelope.

"The gentleman's footman is waiting for a reply, miss."

"Oh, it's from Mr. Worth—an invitation to drive in the park this afternoon." She thought for a moment before saying, "Let me write a quick note of acceptance, and you can take it down to his servant."

When the maid had left, Missy entered the dressing room to choose a carriage dress for the outing. She selected a wool crepe of jonquil with a high neck and long sleeves. The sky was threatening rain, and this would be not only becoming, but also practical if the rain came.

She dressed carefully, feeling a tingle of anticipation as she looked at her image in the glass. It was nonsense, of course. She hardly knew Mr. Worth; it was just all this talk of marriage and love that made the butterflies in her stomach take flight.

She managed a smile for Dulcie, who twisted Missy's hair into a becoming knot on top of her head.

Missy tied on a small straw bonnet adorned with yellow silk roses to complete the ensemble.

When Mr. Worth was announced, Missy was already waiting downstairs in the drawing room. Dillie and Felicity sat with her; they greeted Mr. Worth warmly, but Missy felt a twinge of disappointment when his appearance didn't make her tingle all over. *So much for love,* thought Missy.

"Are you willing to risk it, Miss Lambert?" Mr. Worth was saying—when her attention wandered back to him.

"Risk it?" she inquired politely.

"Going for a drive with the dark clouds looming overhead," he explained patiently.

"I am not made of sugar, Mr. Worth. And if I never went out except when the sun was shining, I would lead a very dull life indeed," she said with a laugh.

Garrett entered in time to hear her comment and to see the smile she bestowed upon his rival. One dark brow arched dangerously, and he observed, "I think it would be best if you postponed your drive, Missy. I have just returned home, and the rain is, I believe, imminent."

"Then we should hurry along, Mr. Worth," she said.

A pleased smirk on his boyish face, Worth looked from one contestant to the other in this battle of wills and offered his arm to Missy.

"By all means," he said, forcing Garrett to step aside for him and Missy to pass by.

When they had gone, Garrett snarled something under his breath and sought the privacy of his chamber.

* * *

"I never realized before how very fascinating these gloves were," said Fitzsimmons Worth when they had completed the first turn around the park. Because of the threat of rain, the path was relatively free of traffic.

Missy hadn't noticed, and now she looked up, puzzled. "I beg your pardon?"

Worth grinned at her and said, "You have been staring at my gloves since we left your house, my dear. I realize they are quite fetching, but I had no idea they could bewitch a young lady. Or perhaps it is my driving skill which you feel you must observe so closely," he offered with an engaging grin.

"I am sorry, Mr. Worth. I did not intend to be rude. Please forgive me."

"You are forgiven, my dear girl. Besides, I have news which I hope will bring a smile to your face."

"News?" she asked, focusing all her attention on him now.

"Indeed, yes. News that I think will please you immensely. While you were, um, out of town, I made inquiries—very discreetly, of course—about holding a match race between your horse and Lord Bagwell's. You know what a gamester he is, and he fancies himself an expert on horseracing."

"Really, Mr. Worth, you should not have mentioned my confidences to anyone!" exclaimed Missy.

"Discreet, remember? I never mentioned your name, thinking you might wish to cry off. I mean, I know what it means to love an animal so much that one might exaggerate his best qualities. We'll say no more about it."

"I did not exaggerate," said Missy.

"Of course not, my dear. As I said, it's forgotten." They drove in silence until they reached the gates of the park.

Mr. Worth sucked on his lower lip for a moment before saying, "It is just such a shame to whistle away a purse of ten thousand."

"Ten thousand pounds?" breathed Missy.

"Quite. But then again, if one has doubts . . ."

"I do not doubt King's ability to beat Lord Bagwell's nag, Mr. Worth," said Missy haughtily. "I fear, however, that my involvement in such a scheme might not be quite proper."

"Oh, is that what is the matter? Why, don't let that trouble you for another moment, my dear. I will take care that the race is not bruited about the ton. That *would* be quite a drawback, but you have my assurance that nothing of the sort will happen."

"But Garrett—"

"Will never find out," he said smoothly. "And you will be the proud owner of ten thousand guineas."

Missy was not as gullible as Mr. Worth thought her and she asked, "Who is putting up the purse, Mr. Worth? If something untoward happened, and King's Shilling did lose, I certainly do not have that kind of cash."

"You don't need to, my dear. There is a group—a very small, discreet group—of men who want very much to take Lord Bagwell down a peg or two, no matter the cost. If you should lose, they will pay the

urse. But if you win, Lord Bagwell has agreed to
ay."

Missy knew King's Shilling could win. She and her
ather had raced against Bagwell's horses many times.
Ie always lost to them, except once, when the stakes
ad cost Missy her best mare, King's dam.

Another problem presented itself even as she
pened her mouth to accept the match.

"Who will ride him? Roberts could have, but I can't
ring him all the way down here for a race that's
oing to take place in secret! Putty could ride him,
ut he's so big, King wouldn't stand a chance of win-
ing."

"It's simple. You ride him," said Worth. *"You* ride
our horse in your match race, and *you* win."

"I don't dare! Right here in London? I don't
are!" she exclaimed. Garrett would disown her—
ot that he did own her. He would be so angry; he
ould never forgive her for doing such an outrageous
ing. Not to mention for allying herself with Worth!

"Not in London, Missy," said Worth, so quietly and
moothly she never questioned his use of her given
ame. "In Wimbledon. It's not far, and I have an
cquaintance with a farm there who owns some
rime meadowland. He has agreed to allow us to
old the race there."

"Wimbledon?"

"Yes. We'll hold the race early in the morning. You
an be back before anyone knows you've gone out
or more than a morning ride in the park."

"Perhaps," she murmured.

"And only think, Missy, with a purse that size, and
stallion who has made his reputation, you can start

your own farm. You won't have to hang on you
guardian's coattails."

Missy knew money was the true reason Mr. Wort
wanted her to race. He didn't really care about he
wish to be independent. But what he said made sens

"You'll keep it very private?"

"You have my word as a gentleman," said Worth

"Then I'll do it."

"Capital! I'll contact Bagwell and set it up."

"When will it be?" asked Missy, trying to be ration
and to keep all her misgivings at bay.

"How about on Monday of next week?"

"But it's already Wednesday!" she exclaimed.

"The sooner it is, the less likely it will become pul
lic knowledge," he warned.

"Very well. I shall simply have to manage it."

"I have every confidence in you, Missy," sai
Worth, smiling down at her.

Suddenly, Missy felt like a little worm with a haw
watching it wriggle along a tree branch. She had be
ter win, she told herself sharply, because Garrett,
he discovered the plot, would never speak to he
again.

When Missy returned from her drive, it was to fin
the ladies of the house at sixes and sevens. Angelica
shy suitor had suddenly appeared and declared h
intentions to Garrett. Having been accepted, he ha
run shouting victoriously into the streets, and hadn
been seen since. Angelica was torn between laughin
and crying, but happiness won out.

Garrett had retreated to his study, but he sent fo

Missy when he learned she had returned from her drive. She was looking decidedly mulish when she entered the room . . . and decidedly beautiful, thought Garrett.

"You look very fetching in yellow, Missy. You should wear it more often," he said, smiling at her.

"Thank you," she stammered, her cheeks turning pink as guilt washed over her. How could she deceive him so? He had been nothing but kind to her and to Felicity. But he was oblivious to her inner dilemma.

"I suppose you have heard about the latest betrothal," he said, indicating the empty spot by his side on the sofa.

"Yes. You have made Angelica very happy by accepting Mr. Neville's offer."

"I suppose they will rub along fairly well," said Garrett. "What of you, Missy? You have been out for an hour with Mr. Worth. Do you have any news to spring on me?"

She nearly jumped out of her skin before she realized he meant romantic news. She shook her head, wondering briefly at the sigh that escaped from Garrett's lips.

"So you don't think you'll bring Worth up to scratch?" he asked bluntly.

"You needn't be so insulting, Garrett. And whether or not Mr. Worth and I have discussed such a possibility is quite beyond your control," she retorted, knowing all the while her outburst was caused by her own guilt and not his off-handed question.

Slowly, Garrett cocked his head to one side, studying his ward intently. "Do not tempt me," he said finally.

"Tempt you? Tempt you to what, Garrett?"

"To exercising my authority over you," he said, favoring her with a decidedly unpleasant sneer. "I am your guardian."

If he was trying to frighten her, he failed miserably. If he merely wished to antagonize her, he had seized upon the very thing.

Her eyes narrowed, and she scoffed, "It would be unwise of you to try such a scheme."

Garrett laughed, but there was no humor in the sound. Never in his life had he been so divided in his mind. On the one hand, he wished to turn her over his knee and spank her soundly. On the other, he wanted to pull her into his arms and kiss her senseless. There was only one more step to take.

"You would choose Worth even if it meant Gretna Green for you, Missy? Because I swear I would never give my consent to the match."

Her fingers tightened to form a fist, just the way Price had taught her, and she pulled back to plant him a facer. Garrett caught her fist easily and twisted her hand behind her back.

"Let go!" she squealed, starting to lash out with her other fist, her feet, her everything.

Garrett brought his lips down on hers. Missy hesitated only a second before throwing her arms around his neck and returning his kiss for all she was worth. The kiss deepened, and Garrett pulled her closer. Missy moaned as his lips left hers and traveled to her neck, sending delicious waves of desire coursing through her body.

Oh, he is *practiced at this,* she thought, wriggling against him.

Too practiced, that old cautious voice warned. Missy began to push against his chest, her efforts sending Garrett slipping from the sofa onto the floor with a thud which instantly brought him to his senses.

Looking up at her from his undignified position, he grimaced and began to apologize, ending with, "If I could undo what just happened, Missy, I would."

What else could she say but, "I agree completely. I think I'll go to my room now." She fled.

Garrett slammed out of the house moments later.

Garrett went straight to his club, hoping the company of rational, jovial men would ease his guilt and disappointment.

How could he have kissed her so? He knew she was an innocent; she had probably never been kissed before, and he had practically seduced her, right there in his study. And as his ward, she was supposed to be under his protection.

Even if he did love her, he should have waited until later to broach the subject—next year when she was no longer his ward. And then only in a gentlemanly manner.

But there was something about Missy that made him forget she was, after all, a gently bred lady. There was an earthiness about her.

Still, there could be no excuse for his behavior!

"Good evening, Garrett. Come to drown your sorrows?" said Ian, throwing himself into the chair next to Garrett's. "Heard about Angelica. Neville's either a saint or a fool. He'll be living under the cat's paw in a month."

"Hmm."

"Understand you're about to have another stroke of luck," said his friend, watching carefully.

Garrett looked over the top of his glass of brandy before lowering it slowly to the table.

"What d'you mean by that?" he asked, proud of himself for speaking so clearly.

"Just that there's to be another one of your petticoat household announcing her betrothal soon."

"The devil you say! I told her she couldn't marry Worth!" he snarled, clambering to his feet.

"Worth? I'm talking about Miss Dill and the admiral. Who the deuce are you talking about?" asked Ian, jumping up and reaching for his friend, pushing him back into his chair.

Garrett sat back, glassy eyed. "I've been a demmed fool."

"If it has to do with women, Garrett, you have plenty of company." Ian signaled a waiter and ordered black coffee for both of them. "I guess this has to do with Missy?"

"Not anymore. If I ever had a chance with her, it's over now. I daresay she can't stand living in the same house with me. Maybe I'll just return to Yorkshire until after the Season. Then she can go and live with you and Felicity."

Admirably, Ian hid his alarm at this possibility, saying only, "That would, of course, leave the girls unprotected in London. I mean, Putty is quite intimidating when they are out shopping, but he can't go to the balls and routs with them, can he?"

"No, I suppose he can't. But devil take me, Ian

've ruined things with Missy for sure. What's a fellow) do?"

"You do have it bad, don't you, old friend?"

"Have what? What the deuce are you talking bout?" demanded Garrett.

"It's as plain as the nose on your face that you're 1 love with the girl. Why not admit it and have one?"

"Love? Me? With Missy? What twaddle!"

"Have it your way. But you still have to make mends, right? Look, it's Wednesday evening. There's lways Almack's. I told Felicity I would be there; that's hy you see me here dressed to the nines, my friend. ou go home and change. There's enough time."

"No, I don't want to do that. If I walked in, and he was waltzing with that tufthunter Worth, I'd call im out!"

"Can't do that, not publicly anyway. Besides, he robably won't even be there. Why don't you go ome and change into knee breeches, and I'll see ou there?" said Ian, rising.

"I'll think on it," said Garrett, setting down the offee and finishing his brandy. Ian shook his head nd walked away.

Garrett ordered another drink before he finally rade up his mind. The thought of Worth and Missy ogether was keeping him from enjoying himself, he easoned, so he might as well present himself at Al-rack's.

A gentleman of Garrett's fortune and social stand-1g would have been welcome any night at Almack's,

but the rules were sacrosanct, and he had neglecte
to follow them.

"I'm sorry, Sir Garrett, but a gentleman must b
properly clothed before I can allow him to enter.
you were wearing the requisite knee-breeches, sir,
would be delighted to admit you," said the extreme
proper doorman.

Nothing Garrett could say would change his min
Finally, Garret shouldered past this paragon only t
come up against two hard chests blocking the er
trance. Not as genteel as their superior, the two foo
men, glowered at him and, each taking an arn
propelled him quickly out the front doors.

"Please come again next week, Sir Garrett," sai
their superior with every evidence of distress at ha
ing to oust him.

Garrett made a rude gesture, jammed his hanc
into his pockets, and sauntered away, ignoring th
jeering crowd who had watched the entire procee
ings with glee.

Had Garrett gone straight home and climbed int
his bed, his case would have fared better, perhaps. A
it was, he stalked into the house, grunted a greetin
to Turtle, and headed straight for his study, wher
he continued to imbibe far more liquor than was h
usual amount.

In the wee hours of the morning, he awoke to th
sounds of the ladies' return and pulled himself o
the sofa, smoothing his wrinkled waistcoat and h
hair, and walking somewhat unsteadily toward th
door of the study.

"A word with you, if you please, Mystique," h
called.

"Mystique? What did you do, Missy?" whispered ngelica.

"I shouldn't go if I were you," added Felicity.

"Rubbish. I have nothing to fear from Cousin Gar-tt," said Missy, smiling for the sake of her sister fore heading toward the study.

Missy was not, however, as sanguine about this en-unter as she pretended. Garrett had obviously shot e cat, or very nearly so. Still, he appeared perfectly ber at the moment, though he was holding his ead.

"Have a cup too much? I only ask because you for-t my dislike of my full name," she commented, pping past him and then walking regally to the fa, perching on the very end as if she didn't intend be there for long.

"I'm fine, but it is kind of you to ask," said Garrett, anaging to ignore the pounding of his head. His dgment was not, however, in the least affected by e liquor he had consumed. He was quite sober.

"You're welcome," said Missy, still very much on er high ropes.

"And no, I hadn't forgotten how much you dislike ing called Mystique, but I have noticed when I call u that, I do get your attention. You never did tell e why you dislike it so—Mystique, I mean. Seems a erfectly good name to me."

"I suppose, but when a girl discovers, quite by ac-dent, that she is named after her father's mistress, doesn't have the same *je ne sais quoi*," she said with erbic honesty.

"Whew, that must have been a facer," said Garrett, lling once again into a brown study.

They sat in silence for a moment before Missy i[n]quired, "Was there something in particular y[ou] wanted to discuss with me, Garrett?"

"Well, yes . . . that is, first of all, I wanted to exten[d] my apologies once more for this afternoon's, er, co[n]tretemps."

"That is kind, but quite unnecessary, I assure yo[u.] If that is all . . ." Missy started to rise, but Garre[tt] touched her hand, and she sank back onto the sof[a,] trembling, though she hoped he was still too muc[h] in his cups to notice.

"There is one other matter." Clearing his thro[at] and his mind, Garrett rose and went to stand by th[e] mantel, resting one elbow on it, trying his best [to] appear composed, even nonchalant. Missy waited p[o]litely, almost indifferently, he thought, so he clear[ed] his throat again and began.

"Missy, I have given our present situation a gre[at] deal of thought in the past few weeks. I might ad[d,] even more so in the past three or four days sin[ce] Felicity and Angelica are now betrothed. I unde[r]stand Miss Dill and the admiral may also be setti[ng] sail on the bed of matrimony."

Missy giggled, and Garrett flushed uncomfortab[ly] and waved his hand as if to wipe away his pomposi[ty.]

"Never mind that," he grumbled. "What I wish[ed] to propose to you, my dear, is . . . well, I wish to pr[o]pose."

Missy's heart leapt to her throat, but she couldn[']t speak, couldn't react to his words. Eyes and mou[th] rounded, she was dumbfounded. Never in her wilde[st] dreams—well, perhaps in her wildest dreams—ha[d] she thought he would offer for her. She had had [a]

a he returned her affection! Affection? Now she
ld call it what it was—her love.

lowly, the spell was broken. Her eyes shining,
ssy opened her mouth to respond, but Garrett was
w pacing back and forth in front of the fire, speak-
 to her, she supposed, though he never looked

"I know I can't offer you the head-over-heels kind
love that Ian offers Felicity. Nor can I offer you
etry like Neville does Angelica. Though, to be hon-
, you would not care to read such drivel, my dear.
t we have much in common, much to offer each
er. You love Lambert Farm and all that entails,
d it is clear you are loath to leave it. And heaven
ows I can use all the help I can get in running the
ate. What's more, when we were in Yorkshire, we
bed along fairly well together," he added, pausing
his perambulations and speaking directly to her.

Any liveliness she had once felt drained from her
dy. And hopes she had once held fled from her
unded heart.

Her head held high, Missy said, "You will under-
nd if I cannot give you an answer tonight. I will
ed a few days to consider your . . . I will need a
v days." She rose and walked slowly to the door,
ud that she had managed to keep her dignity in-
t.

"Of course I understand. It is not a decision to
ke lightly," said Garrett, reeling from her hesita-
n. Couldn't she see that a match between the two
 them was the perfect solution to all their prob-
as? But he said only, "Good night, Missy."

"Good night, Garrett."

* * *

When Missy awoke the next morning, she felt as
she had been out drinking all night. Her stoma
was queasy and she had the headache. Her eyes we
bloodshot and puffy from crying.

She splashed cold water on her face and rubbed
vigorously with a towel. She drew out her favorite o
habit; the color and fit always made her look her be
Without calling for Dulcie, she dressed and made h
way to the stables.

The first hurdle would be convincing Putty that sl
could and should ride King's Shilling in the mat
race. And the first step to convincing the kindly s
vant would be demonstrating to him King's lightnii
speed.

"Good morning, Putty," she said cheerily, forcii
a smile.

"Good morning, Lady Miss. You're out early tl
morning," said Putty. "You just missed the master
guess this warm weather and sunshine makes a bo
want to be out and about."

"Quite right," said Missy, thanking the stars th
she had missed Garrett. And since he had just le
there would be little chance of encountering him
the way out of the mews.

"Could you saddle King's Shilling for me?"

A few minutes later, they were headed out the ga
turning north.

"Excuse me, Lady Miss, but where are we bound

"Oh, I just wanted to get out of town, Putty. I h
Cook pack a little breakfast, and I thought we wou
ride into the country. You don't mind, do you?"

'No, miss. Whatever you wish," said the giant.

They proceeded on in silence, only once more did
tty venture an objection, but Missy assured him they
uld turn around soon. She was relieved when they
ne across the small village church which Mr. Worth
d mentioned was at the corner of his friend's prop-
y.

'Why don't we eat under that tree over there?" she
ggested, pointing to a huge, spreading oak.

Putty eyed the churchyard with its headstones and
stily agreed. He dismounted and opened the gate,
owing her to pass through before he closed it
ain.

Missy kicked out of the stirrup and slipped to the
und unassisted. Putty opened the bag Cook had
t and spread the large, thick cloth on the ground
Missy to sit upon. She began opening napkins,
ealing scones, small meat pasties, and fruit. There
s a bottle of water and one of ale, which she gave
Putty.

'You don't think anyone will mind us havin' a pic-
: here, do you, Lady Miss?" he asked uncertainly
en they were settled.

'Not at all. As a matter of fact, I have permission
be here. This land belongs to a friend of Mr.
rth's. He told me about it."

'Mr. Worth?" said Putty, frowning.

'Yes. He has been a very good friend to me, Putty."

The servant frowned. "I don't think Sir Garrett
es him very much," he said after pondering the
tter for a few seconds.

'No, he doesn't, but sometimes one must make

decisions based on what one knows to be true, r
on hearsay."

Putty studied this for a moment and nodded.

"That is why, Putty, I wanted to come here a
speak to you about a very important matter."

He scooted farther away, frowning nervously.

"Mr. Worth has arranged for me to show everyo
how fast King's Shilling is, but I'm going to need yo
help."

"My help!" he squeaked, looking alarmed.

"Yes. I cannot do this alone. I know you are ve
loyal to Sir Garrett, but if things go well, he will nev
know about the race."

"And if they don't?"

"But they will! They have to!" she added, her voi
tinged with desperation, tears springing to her ey

Never proof against a lady's tears, the gentle s
vant said gruffly, "Tell me, and I'll consider it."

Missy then outlined the plan, emphasizing the
crecy involved and the fact that after Monday, eve
thing could go back to normal.

"But what if you're hurt, miss? What if you lose

"You know what a good rider I am, Putty; I wo
get hurt. And as for losing? That's why I wanted
come out here today and show you just how fast Ki
really is."

"You don't have to prove it to me, Lady Miss,"
said.

"Perhaps not, but if I am asking you to risk yo
job, the least I can do is show you I can't possi
lose; not with King. And when I buy my stud far
you can come and work for me."

He smiled at her youthful enthusiasm, but

ok his head when she insisted that they walk off
ourse. Still, using his long foot as a ruler, they
nted paces along the edge of the meadow, setting
 course. Putty said a quiet, "Go," and Missy urged
 stallion forward. He sprang into action, his long
s churning up turf and distance.

aughing triumphantly as she rode back to the tree
ere he waited, Missy knew she had won him over
mpletely.

"He runs like nothing I've ever seen," said Putty,
bing King's forelock and giving him a piece of
ar. "I don't think I've ever seen anything that could
me close."

"Then you'll help me? You don't have to do much,
t come with me and lend me respectability."

"I'll do it, Lady Miss. But, please, let's try to keep
 secret."

"I promise," said Missy, grinning down at him as
 walked King around the meadow to cool him
wn.

The next morning, Fitzsimmons Worth was waiting
 the corner for them to ride by on their way to
mbledon Common to train for the big race. Join-
 them, Worth kept up a witty commentary on the
evious night's revels, his frivolous chatter serving
 amuse Missy and to allay the giant's fears that he
d formed any unsuitable intentions toward his mis-
ss.

As on the previous morning, King's Shilling exhib-
d a blinding burst of speed. Her cheeks flushed,
r eyes bright and shining, Missy returned to the

tree where Worth helped her dismount. Putty led t
stallion away, though he kept an eye on his mistr
while she prattled on about the big race, Worth
tening indulgently.

From the churchyard, Garrett watched also, l
jaws aching from clenching them so tightly. His fi
instinct had been to reach for his sword. A fitti
place for a duel, Wimbledon. But he had controll
his impulse and now fumed quietly.

Worth picked a piece of grass from Missy's ha
pushing some stray strands away from her brow. T
intimate gesture brought forth a strangled curse fr
Garrett. Finally, he could take no more and, steppi
on a headstone, swung up on his gelding's back, tu
ing him toward London.

Garrett rode to his club and ordered a large brea
fast, which he had to choke down, ignoring the f.
that it tasted like sawdust in his mouth. Even the a
failed to quench his thirst.

Ian, who was still living in bachelor quarters
avoid his sister's domineering tendencies, enter
the dining room when Garrett was finishing his s
ond glass of ale.

"At it kind of early, aren't you?" he asked.

"Devil take you," said Garrett, using his foot
push out the chair on the opposite side of the tal
for his friend to join him.

"Don't mind if I do." He looked at the emp
dishes the footman was clearing and said, "Bring
two of whatever he had."

"Very good, Mr. Emery."

When they were alone again, Ian asked, "Wl
brings you here for breakfast, Garrett? Things goi

adly at home?" Garrett chose to ignore his friend's
question, settling for a glare instead. "Yes, I can see
you would cheerfully run me through, but I am not
he one you should be gunning for, if you'll pardon
my mixed metaphors."

"Well, I can't fight a woman," grumbled Garrett.

"Certainly not," said Ian. "And she is not the
ne you should be angry with, either. I was think-
g perhaps you should look in the mirror for your
rget."

"Confound it! I don't have to listen to this!" said
arrett, but he made no attempt to leave. Finally he
emanded, "What do you mean by that, Ian?"

"Come now, Garrett, you might not have had the
uantity of experience with women that I have had,
ut you are no green boy. You told me what you said
Missy the other night. If I had been her, I would
ve called you out!"

"I made her a very good offer!" protested Garrett.

"A good offer? Are you daft or merely dim-witted?
w would you like it if someone said to you, 'Let's
t married, but only so we can breed horses to-
ther?' "

Garrett had the grace to look shamefaced, but he
sponded, "But that's all she cares about."

'And if you believe that, old boy, you really are
ft. What's more, I think you're deceiving yourself
ou think that's why you want to marry her."

'What do you mean?"

'I mean, Missy is a beautiful woman. If I hadn't
en head over heels in love with Felicity the first
e I laid eyes on her, I would certainly have been
npted to give Missy a tumble—"

"Watch what you say!" exclaimed Garrett.

"There! That's what I'm talking about. Haven't yo
noticed the change in you? How many balls did yo
attend before the girls arrived—and I'm talkin
about proper balls, not those Cyprian affairs?"

"A few," said Garrett.

"And how did they compare with the last one yo
attended with Missy by your side? Rather dull, eh?'

"Hm, I suppose so."

"And just how sorry were you when you discovere
Missy had tagged along on your trip to Yorkshire?
you are honest, I'd wager you were deuced happy
see her, to spend that time with her, and not becau
of those blasted racehorses."

Garrett jumped up, knocking his chair over bac
ward. The footman rushed forward to right it.

Looking around, Garrett sat down again, hunchi
forward to whisper, "Do you think I have a chanc
I mean, there is Worth, always hanging about, he
And I think Missy likes him."

"She may *like* the devil, but it's you she loves."

Garrett pushed away from the table again, a fooli
grin slowly taking hold of his face and not letting g

It faded as he remembered the way she had allow
Worth to smooth her hair.

"She won't have me, you know. I've put my foot
it once too often. She'll take Worth instead. She m
him this morning, and not in the park. Yesterday, t
I'm afraid. All the way out in Wimbledon."

"Ah, so that's where it's to be," murmured Ian

"It? What it?" demanded Garrett.

"The match race between your Missy's King's S
ling and Bagwell's nag."

"The devil you say! So that's what it's all about. But what does Worth have to do with it? And who's going to ride that hellborn stallion of hers?" asked Garrett, though he knew the answer before Ian confirmed it.

"And Worth?" he asked.

"Seems to have arranged the whole. Supposedly, Bagwell has agreed to put up ten thousand against King's Shilling."

"Missy would never agree to that! She'd never risk losing King again. He's more than just a horse to her."

"Nevertheless, that's the *on-dit,*" said Ian. "Bets are running heavily against Missy. I, of course, put a tidy sum on her. I think he'll run his heart out for her, if he's not tampered with."

"You think that's a possibility?" asked Garrett, scowling.

"I think that old derelict Bagwell would do anything for money, and even worse for a stallion such as King's Shilling is rumored to be. And as for the purse, I daresay Worth hasn't told Missy she's putting up her horse."

"But first, you have to let her race that stallion," said Ian. "Forgetting all the rest, Garrett, you have to do something to redeem yourself in her eyes. Actions, as they say, speak louder than words."

"If she is hurt . . ."

"Not to make you feel even worse, and not to carry tales, but according to Felicity, she's already been hurt, Garrett."

"I've been a blasted fool, Ian. Do you think she'll ever forgive me?"

"It could prove pleasant finding out," said the former rake.

"Or very painful," said Garrett with a derisive laugh.

Eleven

That day, Garrett escorted the ladies to a breakfast fresco given by Mr. and Mrs. Milford at their Italian-style villa on the Thames. Having twin daughters marry off, they had been entertaining lavishly that season. The girls, both pretty and lively, were already betrothed, and the breakfast, planned for six weeks, had become an engagement celebration.

There were blue and white striped marquees set on the gently sloping lawns, rowboats on the river, donkey rides for the ladies, bowls on the green grass, and a childish game of blindman's buff which promised to be rather naughty with the gentlemen catching the girls and extracting kisses from them as forfeits. Still, the activities were not scandalous, and everyone enjoyed themselves.

Everyone except Garrett.

Garrett was in agony over his mishandled affairs with Missy. He watched her laugh with a towheaded youth of perhaps twenty and wanted to call the boy out. She allowed Worth to lead her around on the donkey—as if she could not have handled the beast herself! And she even played blindman's buff, wear-

ing the blindfold and running into the embrace
Angelica's betrothed, Mr. Neville.

Ian, with the calm certitude that his beloved w
thinking only of him as she whiled away the afte
noon, sat beside his friend, egging him on in his m
ery.

"If you had only played your cards right," he sa
time and again.

Finally, anger led Garrett to retort cleverly, "Sha
dup!" and he stalked away to nurse his wounds
private.

But Garrett was incapable of staying away for lon
The sight of Missy, dressed in a peach-colored gov
of sarcenet trimmed with blond lace, was like a ton
for him. The gown had the requisite high waist, wi
short, capped sleeves. She wore short gloves made
the same blond lace that trimmed the flounce of h
gown. On her feet were kid slippers, dyed to mat
the gown. No one would guess she was planning
shred her reputation and ride in a match race in on
two days.

As the sun touched the horizon, the girls and th
beaux began to gather around Dillie and the admir
Missy, escorted by Mr. Worth, arrived moments lat
her face flushed with the exertion of bowling.

"Who won, Worth?" asked Ian, glancing sidewa
at Garrett.

"Miss Lambert, of course," said Worth. "She
quite the sportswoman."

With a lingering smile for the admiral, Dillie sa
"Come along, girls. We must rest before dinner a
the dancing begin. Missy, did Dulcie remember
bring your long gloves?"

"Yes, Dillie."

"And, Felicity, what about your headdress?"

"Yes, Dillie."

"Good, then we will excuse ourselves, gentlemen. *tout à l'heure, mes chéries!* See you soon, my dears!" aid the old woman, blowing a kiss toward all the entlemen, but favoring the admiral alone with a flir-tious leer.

"Garrett, my dear boy, I wonder if I might have a ord with you in private," said Admiral Tupperman.

Ian poked his friend in the ribs, but Garrett man-;ed a composed response and followed the older an into the house.

The evening was cool, and Missy pulled the Nor-ich shawl she wore higher, covering her bare shoul-ers. A lavish dinner had been served in one of the uge tents, but the mass of guests had kept the inte-or warm. Now the dancing was about to begin, and e sides had been drawn up on the second tent, lowing the evening breeze to penetrate the heavy nvas. Missy shivered again.

"You'll warm up when you are dancing," said Gar-tt, resisting the temptation to place one arm ound her.

"I suppose so," she replied.

She had been avoiding Garrett since his unfortu-te proposal, and he certainly hadn't mentioned it. erhaps he had been the worse for wear with drink. erhaps he didn't even remember his cold-blooded fer.

"Would you care to dance, Miss Lambert?"

She couldn't refuse him, but if he took her in hi
arms, all her carefully guarded reserve might me
and she might confess all to him—the clandestin
meetings with Worth, the race, even her feelings fo
him. But to refuse would mean she couldn't danc
all night, and that alone might make people specu
late.

"I would love to," she replied, almost wincin
when she realized it was a waltz. His hand in her
his other at her back, made her tingle all over.

They moved as one across the polished woode
dance floor. Garrett did not attempt to speak. H
wasn't at all certain he could. To hold her, to mov
with her in perfect accord—these were the deeds o
his dreams.

Time was running out; their blissful joining woul
soon be over, and he had yet to speak, yet to apolo
gize.

"Missy, when this is all over, we must talk."

Her eyes flew to his face. What did he mean? Ha
he heard about the race?

But there was no anger in his warm regard; instea
she read in his eyes the reflection of the longing i
her own heart. Unsure of her ability to speak, sh
nodded, her lips curving in a tentative smile.

The music ended, and they parted yet again.

Missy spent the remainder of the evening floatin
around the dance floor, holding conversations sh
would never remember, completely unself-consciou
in her happiness.

Felicity taxed her with her abstraction and receive
only a dreamy smile for explanation.

"I don't understand," she said, turning to Ian. "N

ster never enjoys with such unreserved enthusiasm,
uch . . ."

"Bliss?" he supplied, smiling down at his betrothed
nd making her forget all about her sister.

Sunday was spent quietly after attending church
ervices, where the banns were read for Dillie and
he admiral. An impromptu celebratory breakfast fol-
owed, Cook having declared that Miss Dill's be-
rothal was every bit as important as those of the
oung ladies.

Afterwards, everyone retired to their rooms. The
irls did not inquire too closely about where the admiral had gone, but no one saw him leave by way of
he front door. Still, they guarded Dillie's secrets of
he present, just as they had those of her rather
heckered past.

Missy could feel the tension mounting in her shoul-
ers as the minutes ticked by. She had yet to decide
hat habit to wear for the race. A sidesaddle was out
f the question; King would do much better if she
ode astride, so she planned to wear her old breeches
eneath her habit.

Fitz Worth had been as good as his word. It seemed
here had been no leaks about the race, at least not
Society's closely knit circles. Certainly no one had
ade reference to the race at the Milfords' breakfast.

Missy tried to rest, but a nagging ache at her temple
ept her awake. Finally, she dressed and went down
the mews to spoil King with some apple slices.

"You have calmed down so, my beauty; I am so
oud of you," she whispered, stroking his silky neck.

He pushed against her for another tidbit, and sh
laughed. "That's all I have, glutton. You'll have t
wait until tomorrow . . . tomorrow," she repeated
throwing her arms around the stallion's neck an
hugging him.

"Hello, Missy," said Garrett, standing outside th
stall and peering into the gloom.

"Garrett; you startled me," she said, stepping awa
from the big horse.

"Seems I'm always startling one of you," h
quipped. "Planning to go for a ride?"

"No; I just got tired of my own company so
thought I would come out here and visit with King.

"I see. You know, he's remarkably calm. I ca
hardly believe he's the same horse. Maybe you wei
right about him."

"I credit Putty with most of it. He has a calmin
effect on all the horses, I've noticed," said Missy.

"That's why he was always in charge of the horse
that weren't being used in battle. Putty was one
the most important men in the brigade."

"Tell me, Garrett, did you bring the entire brigad
home with you?" asked Missy, smiling at him. "I kno
the footman James was one of your soldiers, and Set
mentioned that he was a drummer, I think."

Garrett grinned and nodded. "I would hav
brought every last one of them home, but some
them stayed in. Still, I have tried to help those wh
came back home find employment. Things are n
easy for a soldier in civilian life."

"Does that include officers?" she asked quietl
suddenly aware of the scent of his cologne mixir

with the smells of the stable. To Missy, it was a heady combination.

"Sometimes, unless one is fortunate enough to inherit a home and a family," he said, smiling down at her.

King's Shilling moved closer and sniffed his hands, looking for another treat. When Garrett raised his hand to stroke the velvety nose, the stallion pivoted and retreated to the far side of the stall.

"He's a little restless," said Missy apologetically.

"Don't worry. I shan't take offense."

"Good," was all she could think of to say. "By the way, Garrett, what was it you wanted to talk to me about?"

At his feigned bewilderment, Missy said, "Last night at the Milfords' you said we had to talk when this was all over." She watched him surreptitiously, but Garrett only shook his head.

"Ah, when this is all over," he said, nodding his head in the most maddening manner. "But it's not over yet, is it?"

Missy blanched. Either he knew about the race or he was being deliberately obtuse. Either way, she had no patience for his games.

"No, Garrett, I suppose it is not. Good afternoon," she said, opening the stall and slipping through. After a moment, she excused herself and returned to the house.

Garrett remained behind, leaning against the door to King's stall, watching her nervous retreat and listening to the restless stallion pace back and forth.

"He's a mite fidgety this afternoon. Easy, big boy,"

said Putty, appearing beside Garrett. The horse quieted immediately.

"Amazing," said Garrett, grinning at his servant. "You still have the touch, Putty."

"Not really, sir. He knows it's time for his supper."

Putty opened the door and entered the stall, pouring the feed into the trough and stepping aside quickly.

"So what time is the race?" asked Garrett, watching Putty carefully.

The giant met his gaze without flinching or surprise.

"Seven o'clock in th' morning, sir. We'll leave by six. Do you plan to stop it?"

"That depends," said Garrett. "Why don't you come out here where we can talk?"

They settled in the tack room, with the door closed, and Garrett began interrogating Putty on all he had seen and heard in the past week.

Finally, the groom commented with uncanny insight, "It seems you're more interested in Lady Miss's encounters with that Mr. Worth than you are about King and the race."

Garrett took a deep breath before admitting, "I hope to make Miss Lambert my wife, Putty. She doesn't know that yet, so I feel certain I can count on your keeping that under your hat."

"Completely," said Putty, grinning happily. "But why are you letting her race, sir? She doesn't realize it, of course, but it's liable t' be a regular carnival in th' morning."

"Very probably, but it means a great deal to Miss Lambert, and I don't want to interfere. I'll be there,

ut in the background. I'm counting on you, Putty
o watch out for her, and for King's Shilling."

"For King?" he asked, frowning.

"I fear there may be some tampering by Missy's
opponent, or even by someone who has bet heavily
or her to lose. I understand the wagers are running
igh against her."

"That's because they haven't seen King run. I have.
He'll win if no one does anything to distract him."

"He has to win, Putty. Missy doesn't know, but
Worth put up King's Shilling against Bagwell's ten
housand."

"Bless me!"

"God bless us all," said Garrett, nodding to the
groom and returning to the house.

Sleep was elusive for everyone who knew about the
big match race to be held bright and early on Monday morning. Garrett, not wanting to spoil Missy's
secret, kept out of the way until he was certain she
had left for Wimbledon Common. Then he saddled
Tucker and followed, taking an out-of-the-way route
o he wouldn't run into anyone heading toward the
ace.

Missy and Putty arrived at the appointed spot well
beforehand, but they were astounded by the car-
iages and men on horseback who clogged the roadway and fields.

"Putty, this has gotten out of hand," she said, not
bothering to whisper amidst the noisy crowd. Garrett
was bound to hear about it!

"Never you mind, miss. Just look at King here;

never seen him so calm and sure of himself. He'll do fine, and so will you. Just remember: don't look back."

"I only hope there is someone behind us who I'm not supposed to look back at." She shook her head and smiled up at the groom. "You did remember to tell Worth not to use a pistol to start the race, didn' you?"

"I told him, miss. Now relax, and ride just like you were at home in Yorkshire. Don't let all these folk alarm you."

"I won't, Putty. I promise."

She spied Fitz Worth striding across the field to ward them, waving his hand wildly to attract their attention.

"Isn't this grand?" he shouted.

"I think it is appalling," said Missy tartly. "This i not at all what you promised me, Mr. Worth,"

"I only told those few men who said they would put up the purse. I couldn't control them or the peo ple they told, now could I?"

Pursing her lips in disapproval, Missy said, "I sup pose not." She had no time for uncharitable thoughts and looked across the opening. "Is tha blue roan over there the gelding Bagwell is racing?"

"That's the one. He's an ugly brute, but he's pretty powerful. Not as fast as King's Shilling, of course."

"Let's hope not. But at least I won't have lost any thing but the match. I can't lose the purse if it's neve been mine in the first place." A troubling though occurred to her, and she asked, "You did not be heavily on me, did you, Mr. Worth?"

"I bet no more than I can afford to lose, my dea

girl," he lied. "Now then, let's get you and King's Shilling to the starting line," added Worth, taking hold of King's bridle before the stallion shook his head and jerked away.

"Very well, my dear," he said nervously. "Just ride him over there."

"That's Miss Lambert," snarled Putty as he shouldered roughly past Worth.

Amazingly, the crowd parted to allow them passage, and the noise began to subside. King's Shilling looked left and right, prancing daintily, but he didn't appear to be overly bothered by the carnival atmosphere until someone waved a driving whip at him. As he reared up on his hind legs, Missy held tight until Putty could calm the nervous stallion.

Garrett left Tucker tied to a tree in the churchyard and forced his way through riders and carriages toward the starting post, his black scowl keeping anyone from protesting. His plan to stay away until after the race was forgotten when he saw the stallion dancing on his hind legs. All he could think of was getting to Missy.

Worth patted Missy's hand and smiled up at her. His other hand slipped beneath the stallion's blanket. Putty's huge hand shot out and caught Worth just below the elbow, forcing him away from King's Shilling.

"Here now, what's this?" asked Putty, prying Worth's fingers open.

"I saw that burr and was just pulling it out. We don't want King to feel any discomfort, do we?" said Worth, flexing his hand.

"No, we don't," said the giant, standing over Worth

until he smiled nervously and hurried away, stepping onto a carriage to start the race.

"On your mark . . . get set . . . go!" yelled Worth, lifting a pistol and firing it before Missy could protest.

The report of the gun sent King rearing and bucking; the crowd, most of whom had wagered against Missy, roared with excitement. The noise behind him now, King leapt forward, sensing the chase as he set his eyes on the roan's rump. Missy urged him onward, using only her knees and her voice.

The horses rounded the first turn neck and neck. Missy hunched down as low as she could, calling to her horse. His ears flat back, he leapt forward, increasing his speed in response to her soft pleas. Just as they completed the last turn and were heading toward the finish line, King's Shilling pushed ahead, leaving the spent roan in his wake.

Recalling Putty's instructions, Missy refrained from looking back, but the temptation was great. She could hear the roan's pounding hooves on the right, but he couldn't catch King's Shilling, and they flew past the finish line leaving no doubt as to who won the race. At the end, the spectators were a blur, but Missy had the impression that Mr. Worth had been screaming obscenities when they crossed the line. *Absurd,* she thought. He must have been cheering.

Missy turned King and brought him back to the makeshift winner's circle, formed by the mass of spectators. Putty hurried to the stallion's head, and she slipped to the ground, feeling strong hands grasp her waist. She whirled to protest, but the words died in her throat and a hot blush rose to her cheeks as she stared into Garrett's ashen face.

"Putty, take care of the stallion," directed Garrett, pulling her away from the circle. "Little fool," he muttered.

Nervous, Missy turned back to the crowd, but they were busy settling their wagers and untangling the mass of carriages for the drive back to town.

"Oh, there's Mr. Worth!" she called.

Fitzsimmons Worth, an ugly look on his face, started toward Missy, so intent on her he didn't notice Garrett just behind her.

"We won!" she shouted, feeling it only right to share the victory with the one who had arranged the match.

"Won? The devil you say! You've ruined me!" he exclaimed, grabbing her arm and pulling her roughly forward.

"What are you talking . . . Oh! Garrett, don't!" she protested when Garrett's fist crashed into Worth's jaw, sending him reeling.

"Don't? You have no idea what you're talking about!" Garrett shouted, his fear for her turning to anger.

"Garrett, I . . . Oh!" she shouted when Worth charged Garrett and received an uppercut to the jaw, lifting him off the ground and flying backwards to fall limp and unconscious in the dirt.

"Humph!" grunted Garrett in satisfaction.

"Garrett, you may not like Mr. Worth, but he is my friend . . . Garrett! Put me down this instant!"

Garrett stopped and dropped her from his shoulders, making her teeth rattle.

"So you want the likes of Worth for a friend," said

Garrett. "You're welcome to him. And here come
another one just like him."

"Bagwell?" she asked.

"He wants to give you his note; at least he hono
his wagers. Why don't you ask him what would hav
happened if you had lost, Missy? Just ask him," h
challenged.

Eyes flashing with righteous anger, Missy turned t
the old man, accepted the note, and then aske
tight-lipped, "What if I had lost?"

"Lost? You know good and well what would hav
happened, Miss Lambert. King's Shilling would hav
been mine again. But you didn't, damn you. Tell m
would you consider selling him?"

"No, my lord. King is not for sale. Not now—n
ever."

Grumbling oaths under his breath, the old ma
moved away.

Missy turned back to Garrett, frustrated that sh
owed him an apology, but willing to make amend
all the same.

Garrett, however, was nursing his bruised knuckl
and was in no mood for a simple apology.

"I am sorry, Garrett," she said.

"And so you should be!" he snapped. "Just tell m
one thing, Missy. Do you love this miserable excus
for a man?" he asked, kicking at the dirt where Wort
was just then trying to sit up.

"Garrett! This is not the place—"

"Hell and blast! How the deuce can this not be th
right place? It's not like it's Almack's or any oth
respectable place!"

"Garrett! Your language!" she objected, but he ignored her.

"All I want is an answer, Mystique Lambert. I'm tired of all the games. Which one of us is it to be? Do you want to marry me or Worth?" he continued.

"Maybe I should marry him!" she cried.

"Marry me?" squeaked the horrified Fitzsimmons Worth, scrambling to his feet and backing away.

Mortified, Missy turned and fled, but Garrett caught her up and turned her in his arms.

"What is this, Missy Lambert? Playing the coward?"

"Leave me alone, Garrett!" she commanded.

But Garrett teased, "Leave you alone, my love? Just look at the trouble you get into when I do leave you alone."

Missy scowled at him, her gaze troubled as she looked into his eyes. "Maybe I *should* marry you. Just to teach you a lesson," she said, but her tone lacked the bravado of her words.

Garrett lowered his head and kissed her lightly on the lips. Then pulling her close, he rested his chin on the top of her head and breathed in the essence of her scent, holding her safe in his arms, letting his fingers revel in the feel of her long, silken hair.

"Let's get away from here," he said huskily, guiding her toward the churchyard. Missy stole a glance around. Everyone had left; they were quite alone except for the three horses and Putty, who was busy tending to King's Shilling.

"You know, Missy, I haven't forgotten that awful proposal I made to you last week."

Eyes wide, Missy leaned back in his embrace to look into his face. "It really was quite dreadful, Garrett."

"It was more than dreadful; it was stupid and untruthful. I want to marry you, but not because you know how to run Lambert Farm. I love you, Missy; that's the pure and simple truth."

When she smiled, it was as if the sun had peeked out from the clouds, and she said, "I love you, too, Garrett."

He leaned against a tree and pulled her against him. Lifting her chin with one finger, he kissed her, long and slow. Missy melted into him, feeling at peace for the first time in years. Forgotten were all the struggles of her father's illness, his death, his stupid will.

Garrett raised his head, watching her as she blinked slowly, dreamily. "A penny for your thoughts, my sweet."

"Hmm? Oh, I was just thinking how thankful I am that Papa wrote that stupid will."

"So am I. So am I," said Garrett, kissing her again.

Fat, heavy raindrops began to penetrate the cover of the tree, and they reluctantly called Putty to bring the horses.

"Ride ahead on King's Shilling, Putty, and tell them we'll be wanting hot water and hot drinks when we get home," said Garrett.

"Very good, sir," said the groom, favoring his master and mistress with a delighted smile. "And may I be the first to wish you happy?"

"Thank you, Putty," they said in unison.

Garrett threw Missy into Tucker's saddle and then mounted Horse. Alone again, they continued along the tree-lined lane, riding slowly, ignoring the gentle rain.

Garrett's brow wrinkled, and Missy asked, "What's the matter, Garrett?"

"I just realized you never answered my question."

Missy grinned and chided, "That is because you never asked it, my dear."

" 'Pon my honor, not properly betrothed and I'm already living under the cat's paw," teased Garrett, but he stopped Horse and Tucker. Taking Missy's hand in his, he asked, "Will you do me the great honor of becoming my wife, Miss Lambert?"

"Are you certain?" she asked, almost afraid to believe in her good fortune, almost afraid to ask the question for fear he would renege.

"Of course I am certain, you ninnyhammer," he said.

"Garrett, that is not the way . . . oh . . . hmm . . ."

"Well, will you?" he asked when he had finished tormenting her with his kiss.

"Yes, Garrett. I will marry you."

"Good. Now that that's settled, let's get out of this miserable weather. Race you back to town!"

"Go!" shouted Missy, urging her mare forward.

"That's cheating!" he laughed, setting out in hot pursuit.

ABOUT THE AUTHOR

Donna Bell lives in Texas with her husband of twenty-eight years and her son, who is attending a nearby university. Her two married daughters and new granddaughter also live in the area. When not writing, Donna teaches high school French. Other pastimes include cross-stitching, reading, and traveling. She loves to hear from her readers; you may contact her through Zebra Books or E-mail her at: dendon@gte.net.

More Zebra Regency Romances